Awards Received

2014 Moonbeam Book Award	**Eric Hoffer**
Hollywood Book Festival	**Eric Hoffer, Montaigne Medal**
Beach Book Festival	**Reader's Views Reviewers Choice**
New York Book Festival	**Great Northwest Book Festival**
Eric Hoffer	**London Book Festival**
Los Angeles Book Festival	**San Francisco Book Festival**
The San Francisco Book Festival	**Beach Book Festival**
Great Northwest Book Festival	**Hollywood Book Festival**
Feathered Quill	*Indie Excellence Awards*

Other Accolades for 84 Ribbons

Dance Spirit Magazine 'Pick of the Month' for April 2014.

YA ForeSight, ForeWord Magazine. *84 Ribbons* selected for showcase article. One of five young adult novels showcased for Spring 2014 in *The Risky Business of Growing Up*.

 Act 4

The Continuing Friendship
of Lynne & Marta

Paddy Eger

When Does a Trilogy Become a Series?

When the main characters ask for more of their lives to be shared. I thought I was finished with Marta and Lynne after three books: 84 Ribbons, When the Music Stops, and Letters to Follow. I was wrong. They had more to say to me and to you, so Act 4 was set in motion. Last November, during NANOWRIMO (Novel Writing Month), more of their story sent me back to them. They were finally ready to step into adulthood with all its added responsibilities and changes, including stepping away from their parents and depending on themselves to make life-changing decisions. I hope you'll enjoy this end to their life stories. I'll now leave them alone to move forward without my prying into their lives—unless they call out to me again.

Friends are connected heart to heart

Distance and time can't break them apart

—Unknown

Billings, November 1959

*L*ynne brushed her rain-drenched hair out of her eyes as she emptied the gas can into her stubby Nash Rambler's tank. "Should've remembered the gauge wasn't accurate," she grumbled to herself. "Its been five months since I filled it. Shouldn't have expected a miracle."

Now she'd be late, something Damien didn't tolerate, especially from the 'reformed' Lynne, the world-traveling dancer returning home. Could anything else go wrong this first week back? She hoped not.

Embarrassed by her ragged appearance, she toweled her wet hair and scurried into her practice clothes. Hopefully, next week she'd be able to purchase pointe shoes and new leotards. Time to speak with Damien about her situation—the last thing she wanted to do.

She slipped into the room ten minutes late, took the empty space closest to the entry door, and nodded toward Damien. His eye-roll response in her direction caused everyone to follow his gaze and home in on her. So much for sneaking in without being noticed. She braced herself for Suzette, who would no doubt take every opportunity to mention her tardiness with gusto.

Muscle memory took over as she dropped into traditional warm-ups: *plies, battements, ronde jambs* on both sides. Head rotations matched arm extensions and body angles in harmony with the piano's accompaniment. Deep breaths and the joy of movement blocked everything outside the practice room. For a moment, she closed her eyes. *How can anyone not feel the release of soothing music?*

With warm-ups completed, Lynne moved to the back of the room to observe the *corps de ballet* choreography for *Sleeping Beauty*, the ballet she'd missed while she'd been in Europe. The company, midway through their performances, had few kinks left to work out. Knowing Damien, however, she'd almost bet he'd added amazing personal variations, and provided solo opportunities to showcase his dancers.

She could hardly wait to get back to performing. When she'd checked in with the office yesterday, they informed her she would be wearing black clothes and taking on backstage duties until the current performances ended, an assignment she expected. Although lacking in creativity, it would be an easy job: gather up whatever stray costume items hit the floor on the left wing to prevent dancers from slipping or falling. It would also keep her a part of the ballet, even if she wasn't onstage.

Suzette's sloppiness and her me-me attitude became even more apparent from backstage. Lynne shook her head. She'd wager a hundred dollars and win that Suzette's actions were intentional, but nobody would take her bet. Everyone except the new dancers knew she did only what benefitted her. Unfortunately, the newbies would learn the hard way to keep their distance.

⌒⌒⌒∘⌒⌒⌒

Midday break, Lynne paced outside Damien's office in lieu of eating lunch. She couldn't afford to join the others, so it didn't matter. At least water was free. Confessing her financial crisis to the company director upset her, but it was better than when Madame Cosper had humiliated her in the past.

Poor woman. Confined to a wheelchair with round-the-clock care, Madame had transitioned from powerful director of the Intermountain Ballet Company to powerless stroke victim. She didn't adapt well to losing control. Lynne frowned. *Does anyone really adapt to such a change?* She'd plan a visit soon so the director could yell at her and send her away like old times. A rueful smile slid across her lips. That should briefly stir the former director's pleasure.

Damien opened his door and nodded for her to enter. He checked his watch as he sat on the edge of the desk, waiting for her to speak.

She straightened and composed her thoughts. "I apologize for being late again. I'm having a bit of a car issue. All my money was in a fund Leo handled. He took it with him when he left me stranded in Portugal. I have exactly ten dollars and eighty-two cents until I get my paycheck from the ballet company. Since Leo also has my ballet bag, I have only this one set of practice clothes and shoes. I'm hoping you'll approve my getting new clothes, ballet slippers, and two pairs of pointe shoes from the costume mistress. You can take it out of my check."

"That can be arranged, but it won't help your tardiness, will it?"

"No. I plan to park my car and walk in until I can afford gas. I also owe rent and need to buy food once I get paid. Maybe, since I'm not dancing in performances, I could work weekend mornings at the dance academy and—"

"That's a good idea. You can help select the young dancers for the upcoming *Nutcracker* season." Damien glanced at his watch. "I'll authorize Rose to give you clothes and shoes. While you're there, have her check your measurements. You appear to have lost weight since June. I

imagine there's a story in there somewhere."

She nodded. "Thank you for helping me. I won't be late again."

Damien bit his lip and half-smiled as he opened the door for her to leave. "Hope not."

Just like it had happened before she left for France, opening the office door revealed a hunched over, surprised Suzette, stumbling against the wall next to the door. Lynne scowled as the eavesdropper scurried away. The company troublemaker hadn't changed.

Watching performances from the wings gave Lynne the opportunity to observe her fellow dancers' strengths, perseverance, and grace. She also witnessed the nonchalance of a few when handling their costumes or respecting the backstage crew. They removed every tiny scrap and every dropped hairpin to keep the floor safe for dancers *en pointe*, making turns, or leaning gracefully to one side.

It also taught her that stagehands did a lot more than pick up stray items so dancers wouldn't fall. They also maintained sets, adjusting fly rails, back drops, and leg curtains. Plus, they stayed in contact with the lighting technicians at the back and top of the house. All the while dressed in black to promote their near-invisibility in the darkened backstage area, they were mostly ignored by the dancers. She frowned at the lack of gratitude displayed for their hard work. *Everyone should take a turn working backstage at least once to appreciate how much is done to support their on-stage presence.*

Seeing the orchestra pit from this perspective made her more aware of how carefully the conductor synchronized the music with the movements of the dancers. Prima ballerinas like Patrice kept their pace steady to work in consort with the conductor. Lynne shuddered when she thought of how Suzette would handle being a soloist. She'd make the maestro crazy and probably cause defection of orchestra members by her erratic movements and tempo changes. *Would they be intentional?* Blinking back tears when considering the terrible impact this would have on the ballet company, she feared it might actually be deliberate.

The last performance of *Sleeping Beauty* ended Sunday evening to a packed house. As a gold circle subscriber, her boyfriend Noel would attend the celebration for patrons after the final performance of each ballet. Lynne, however, stayed behind to help the costume shop crew hang and check the outfits for damage. Next week, they'd be sorted, cleaned, mended, and put in storage before moving on to prepare the Nutcracker costumes.

When the work was finished in the costume shop, Lynne headed home and sat in Mrs. B's common room, waiting for Noel. The clock ticked passed eleven, then eleven-thirty. Following his confession when they first met about not enjoying after-parties, she wondered if his attitude had changed after she explained their importance. Because he didn't seem to need his ego stroked like many patrons did, it didn't seem likely he stayed for that reason. His family paid more than their fair share in support of the arts and also provided the champagne many patrons guzzled like water, so he didn't stay because he needed to establish his right to be there. She smiled a little. Her words must have made a difference.

At eleven forty-five, Noel knocked. As soon as she opened the door, he wrapped her in a huge hug before they sat down on the couch.

"Hey you. Missed you at the after-party."

"Sorry. As a temporary stage crew member, I wasn't invited. Not that I missed acting nicey-nicey."

Noel laughed. "Ah, yes. When I met you, I remember you were hiding out with your shoes off."

"True. You were amazingly kind, even after I insulted your family's providing the champagne."

"You know how I feel about such functions."

Lynne leaned against Noel. "How do you feel about after-after functions like this?"

He kissed her cheek and smiled. "These are my favorite. However, you'd have enjoyed tonight's party. Damien received endless praise for his adaptation of the ballet. But instead of basking in the multitude of compliments, he thanked everyone for attending and supporting the company. Madame Cosper would have relished being acknowledged and made herself the center of attention."

They sat holding hands and talking about his kids camp and her upcoming *Nutcracker* tour and performances. "Will you have time to come out to the ranch before you get embroiled in *Nutcracker*?"

"How about I come out tomorrow?"

"How 'bout I build a fire and have Cook prepare your favorite foods?"

Lynne tapped her chin and smiled. "How 'bout we spend most of my visit snuggling?"

A big grin spread across his face. "I'll consider it."

Lynne poked him in the ribs and leaned into his hug. *How have I been so lucky to get to know such a kind, lovable cowboy?*

Monday started out windy and rainy as Lynne drove to Noel's family ranch. Chilled to the bone, she hurried inside to find a crackling blaze in the fireplace, warm blankets on the couch, and Noel waiting for her with a big smile on his face. She snuggled next to him as they talked and drank Cook's coffee while they nibbled on his delicious snacks.

"Are you ready for the *Nutcracker*?"

"Yep. We'll prep over the next two weeks, then tour and be back in town to perform through Christmas Eve. It will be a busy few weeks but then we have a break until the new year."

"What are you holiday plans? Going home to Trenton?"

"Nope. We're still at a stand-off. I'll spend Christmas Eve at the boarding house, but no plans after that."

"Should I ask about that stand-off?"

"Nope."

"Can I steal you away for a few days?"

"Absolutely!"

"Have you tried talking to your mother?"

"No. She knows where I am."

Noel stared at her but made no further comment. After a few seconds, he stood, added wood to the fire, and sat back down beside her.

Tears slid down her face. Putting his arm around her, he waited for her to speak. She remained silent. He gently pulled her closer, watched the fire crackle, and listened to the pitch pockets burst. Lynne's breathing slowed; she'd fallen asleep leaning on his shoulder.

At lunch they feasted on Cook's chili and cornbread. Lynne perked up and began telling him about working for the dance academy. "I'll make a bit of money so I can start paying my bills and buy more than a gallon of gas at any one time."

"I can loan you money if you'll take it."

"I can't. You've done enough. You got me home from France. I can never repay you for that."

"I don't expect you to repay me."

"I know, but I need to figure this out by myself. It's my problem, and I want to fix it."

"Do you have enough gas to get home and to drive to the company? You have noticed it's getting colder, and we'll have snow any day."

"I'll park my car for now, except to drive out to see you. Once I get paid, I'll fill the tank."

"Do you know how to wrap presents and add fancy bows?"

"Of course. Why?"

"I can't let you drive around on fumes. If you'll wrap Christmas presents for me, I'll fill you gas tank."

"I—"

"Lynne, I'll give you a choice. Wrap presents for me or stay here until January."

"Noel... I ... Okay. When do you want me to start?"

He kissed her forehead, jumped to his feet, and disappeared down the hall. He returned with an armload of boxes and bags, Christmas-themed wrapping paper, ribbons, tape, and scissors. "How's now? I've

already bought gifts for the ranch hands, Cook, my business partners, and my family."

"It's only the middle of November."

"So?"

Lynne laughed. "Most guys shop on December twenty-third."

"Guess I'm different."

"You certainly are. Looks like I'll be here all afternoon if you expect them all wrapped before I leave."

"Sounds good to me. I'll go fill your tank. You do know I'm getting the better end of the deal. With gas at twenty-five cents a gallon and your small gas tank, you're getting paid about ten cents a package."

Monday evening at Mrs. B's extended the calm she'd had with Noel, especially now that Carol skipped many evening meals with the boarders. Their sharing of the upstairs bathroom was hectic enough without her snooty comments or her nose buried in her plate at dinnertime. The rest of the boarders had become Lynne's friends when she used to visit Marta at Mrs. B's. Without Carol, dinner conversations circled the table, jumping from topic to topic like in a large family—sharing their day, funny anecdotes, and asking questions.

Faith rented a room since August and fit in as though she'd lived there for years. Mrs. B shared that she worked as a psychologist. "She's also a fitness nut, so you and she will have lots in common. You need to check out the changes to the basement and work out how you two ladies will share the space."

Hmm. That's new. Lynne pursed her lips. *Marta had had the basement to herself. Hopefully, Faith won't be like Carol. I'll know soon.*

The young women met downstairs after dinner. Lynne scanned the rearranged space. A stationary bike sat in the small alcove. A punching bag dangled from a rafter and a small couch marked off the area. A dartboard hung on the wall. Hand weights and other small exercise equipment filled a box tucked under a square table that held the record player and a tape recorder.

"Wow, Faith. You are really into fitness. I'm impressed."

"I hope to become a permanent part of the emergency team after I finish courses at the college. I'll need to pass rigorous fitness tests." She paused for a moment. "Mrs. B thought we could share this space."

"I think we can. I need the open area, my practice barre, the record player and tape deck. Does that work for you?"

"I can be flexible. What hours do you need?" Faith asked.

Lynne stared off into space, squinting while thinking. "If I can use a one-hour weeknight block and two, two-hour blocks on weekends when we're not performing, I'll be fine. Maybe we could hang up a calendar and sign-up each week."

"That works for me. Feel free to use my equipment anytime. Do you play darts?"

"I've tried, but I'm not very good. Maybe you can give me some pointers."

"Sure." Faith laughed. "Would you'd like to join my dart club? We play in the backroom at Daniel's Bar and Diner on Mondays. It's a fun group. We drink a little beer, play darts, and have a few laughs."

"I'm underage, but maybe they'll let me play. I'll check it out. Thanks!"

They hung the month's calendar, filled in the next two weeks, and headed upstairs. As Faith turned into her room on the main floor, Lynne stepped into the kitchen. She found Mrs. B putting the last of the dishes away, a job Lynne had planned to do for her.

"Sorry I'm too late to help you tonight. Faith and I made a plan. It's posted so everyone can read it."

"I knew you'd work it out. I think you'll find Faith to be a great friend."

"I agree."

Mrs. B hung her damp towels and put the teakettle on the stove. "Care for a cup of tea?"

Lynne nodded. "Thanks. I, ah, need to ask a favor or two."

While they sat at the kitchen worktable, Lynne cleared her throat, deciding how to frame her requests. "I'm wondering if you still have the old bike Marta used. Might I borrow it to get to the ballet company?"

"Has your car broken down?"

"No. It's my money that's broken. I have nine dollars and forty-five cents. I bought a loaf of bread, peanut butter, and deodorant today. I can't even afford twenty-five-cent gas until I get paid. Noel filled my tank earlier today. I never know when I might need a few bucks for something, so I'm trying to be cautious."

"Oh, Lynne. It's a shame about your uncle absconding with every-thing. Of course, you can use the bike. Just get the tires checked before you ride very far. Is there anything else you need?"

"Wax paper bags for sandwiches. I'll be taking my lunch with me until…" Lynne chuckled. "Maybe until forever."

"Take whatever you need. The fruit in the bowl on the worktable is always there for the taking. I know you're doing your best. I could lend you money; would that help?"

"Thanks, but I can't take money from you. I already owe you No-vember's rent and December's is coming soon. I want to get this all straightened out on my own as soon as possible."

Lynne and Mrs. B sat in silence, sipping their tea and listening to the faint sounds of horses and gun shots on the television in the common area where James and Shorty sat watching, *Gunsmoke,* their favorite program. When both women stood and took their cups to the sink,

Lynne gave Mrs. B a hug. "Thanks! See you in the morning."

Upstairs, Lynne lay on her bed and stared at the ceiling. Her home-coming in Billings had been so welcoming. *Why can't my family be supportive like Mrs. B? I would like to be in contact with them and share my touring experiences. I want to hear them say they love me. Now it's up to them to resume a relationship with me, and I don't know if they ever will.*

Tears trickled down her face as she climbed under her covers. *Thank goodness I have Marta, Mrs. B, and Noel who believe in me.*

Billings, November

ynne remembered Damien's *Nutcracker* choreography from last year's performances. Much as she loved the ballet, however, she didn't want the role of Mother Ginger. Frowning, she weighed her options. Because she'd be helping the dance academy students, it appeared she'd been pre-selected to play that role—which meant she would not be able to audition for some of the solos she'd hope for. Impressing Damien with her improved skills would have to wait for another opportunity. She sighed. At least she remained part of the company.

Madame Cosper had hired Gretchen Ott to manage the dance academy the moment she retired from a California ballet company. Damien, as head of their board of directors, continued to support her excellent work with the students. Her skills and professionalism made her the perfect person to oversee the development of dancers who'd possibly join the company over the next few years.

Lynne only met her in passing when she'd helped the four little girls earn scholarships to the academy. She and Marta had worked with the children on their own time in Mrs. B's basement. When the ballet company needed child substitutes in the *Nutcracker*, the little girls filled in admirably and were now enrolled, free gratis, for as many years as they cared to take lessons.

Assigned to work again with the younger students, Lynne smiled broadly when she walked into the children's practice and saw three of her young friends. Carmen, Lucy, and Tracy gasped and started to step away from the practice *barre* where they'd begun warmups. Lynne put her finger to her lips and shook her head. Quickly, they stepped back, smiled, and took sneak peaks Lynne's direction.

Observing the interchange of smiles, the instructor called her over. "Lynne, I presume?"

Lynne nodded and curtsied.

"It appears you know some of my students."

"Yes. Sorry if I've distracted your class."

"It's a good test for them. We're working on staying focused. Perhaps when we divide up the dancers for specific directions, you'd like to work with them. We're about to start giving out Nutcracker parts."

"Thanks, I'd love to see how they've progressed."

Working with the three students she knew plus two others excited her. They reminded her of herself when she was young and enthusiastic. Was she still excited about dancing? Oh yes. Now she needed to prove to Damien and this instructor she belonged in the company, as well as assisting here at the dance academy. This opportunity represented her willingness to commit herself to the future of Billings' Intermountain Ballet Company.

Billings, November

When Lynne entered the kitchen early Wednesday morning to make her lunch, she found a paper lunch sack with her name on it and a note:

> *Thought you needed a good start this AM.*
> *Had leftover roast so I made you a sandwich,*
> *tossed in cookies. Pick a fruit from the basket on*
> *the table. Have a wonderful day!*

Tear flooded her eyes. *Where else could I have lived where someone actually cared about me? Not many places and certainly not with my family. I'll remember this kindness for a very long time.*

Her days at the ballet company returned to normal: morning warmups followed by group sessions for the various Nutcracker dances and afternoons dedicated to ensemble pieces or helping dance academy students. For herself, the *Nutcracker* had been a continuous gift of favorite music and choreography from age seven onward.

The current waltzes brought back new waltzes she learned on her summer tour in France. She'd heard rumors that Damien wanted to perform Khachaturian's *Masquerade Waltz* in the spring, but she'd yet to see details for the season. *It might be on the dressing room bulletin board. I'll look. Cheryl must have shared Masquerade Waltz with him. She did send me home with the music.*

Ah, France. So many great memories, so many train trips, so much history, so many venues. Maybe the new first-year or even second-year dancers would want to apply. She'd help them if they were interested, remembering that Damien took great pride in having her represent the Intermountain Ballet Company.

At noon Lynne bundled up and sat on the front steps. A brisk wind hurried around the corner, so she moved to a sheltered area to enjoy the lunch treats Mrs. B had packed for her. After today, she'd be back to PB and J, which was okay with her. Nothing beat PB and J for saving money and for making a yummy sandwich.

Jer hurried up the steps and slid in next to her, shivering and blowing puffs of hot breath into her face. "Thought it was you. Hiding out?"

"No. Escaping for a few minutes of quiet to enjoy my lunch."

"You could have joined us at The Dude Ranch. Suzette wasn't there."

"Can't. I'm broke until payday. Don't ask. It's a long story."

Jer nodded, sat back, and closed his eyes. "This is a great place to escape for a few minutes."

"That's why I'm here. How long do we have?"

Jer checked. "Seven minutes. You need a watch."

"Not in my budget." Lynne hopped up. "Got to go. Can't be late even one minute after my earlier car problem. I'm working at turning over a new leaf."

Jer followed her. "That I gotta see."

Lynne entered the boarding house through the kitchen after parking the bike back in the garage. She grabbed a cookie and a banana from the worktable and headed upstairs for a shower. It was moments like

this that she missed Marta. Two years ago, they'd debrief about their day with Madame and Damien, chat about Suzette's latest troublemaking, and wonder why she wasn't fired from the company for her unprofessional antics. *Maybe I'll ask Jer his opinion of Suzette one of these days.*

At five o'clock Lynne hurried to the kitchen to help Mrs. B as repayment for her delicious lunch. She washed the potatoes, made a salad, and set the table. Then she sliced the pie into eight even pieces and ate the bits of crust leftover in the pie pan after dishing the slices onto dessert plates. Having someone else cook meals was a pleasure she didn't take for granted after spending much of the last two years attempting to cook for herself. Mrs. B was a better cook than her own mother.

Almost against her better judgement, she thought back to the last time she saw her parents. It had been in June, as she was leaving for France. For once, their time together remained relatively peaceful. *Why can't all our times together be like that? Why do they continue to think dancing is a phase I'll outgrow? Will they ever understand it's my passion as well as my career for years to come?* She shook her head and exhaled slowly.

As soon as dinner finished, Faith headed downstairs to use the space, leaving Lynne to finish sorting her last move-in boxes. Maybe she'd call Marta or Noel or both of them. First, she'd get through the boxes and then…

A knock sounded at her door. "Lynne?"

When Lynne opened it, Mrs. B handed her a letter. "This came for you yesterday. I guess you didn't see it. Thought it might be important."

Lynne recognized the handwriting. Her heart fluttered with anticipation. The letter was from her mother. *Is this good or bad? Should I open it now or wait? Can I ignore it? No.* She sat down in the rocking chair by the window and opened the envelope.

> *A post card. How rude! How could you treat your family with so little respect?*
>
> *I've heard from Leo. He says you walked away and left him without his passport or any travel money. We didn't raise you to be a thief!*
>
> *In case you are wondering, he is okay. He's with his new friends and traveling through Italy for another few weeks. I'm so embarrassed by your actions and your attitude. I can't show my face to anyone in the family.*

An unexpected cry escaped Lynne's lips as she crushed the letter in her hand. How could her mom believe she'd do that to anyone, even Leo? *He'd* taken the money. *He'd* left *her* almost penniless in Portugal. She'd walked and hitchhiked her way back to Paris and then called her parents for help, which they didn't or couldn't give her. They didn't even offer any suggestions about where she might seek assistance. *If it wasn't for Noel, I have no idea where I'd be right now.*

She paced her room, then went back to unpacking her belongings and stuffing them haphazardly into drawers. After more pacing, she rushed down to the basement to see if Faith had finished her workout.

The telltale scent of sweat filled the space around Faith's equipment, but the room was empty. Lynne paced the entire area, muttering to herself about her family believing Leo and not even listening to her side of the story. He was the family's consummate liar and party animal. He left a trail of unreliability, broken promises, and emotional debris on whatever he touched—to say nothing of outright theft. She knew deep down she should never had trusted him, but his offer to pay her way to

Europe had seemed too good to pass up. She'd learned a hard lesson. What now?

Lynne pressed out the crumpled letter and reread it. Her heart pumped wildly. Her head and chest ached. *How can I ever go home again? Do I even want to? What if Dad gets sick again? Will I break down and go home to see him?*

Standing in front of Faith's dartboard, she tugged a dart out and used it to hang the letter over the center of the board. Then she picked up the rest of the darts and began firing them at the bullseye, hitting the now-hidden rings of the board with every shot. With pangs of painful satisfaction, she took a final look at the dart-riddled letter, turned slowly, and trudged up the stairs.

Marta sat in her tiny living room with a cup of peppermint tea while putting the final touches on her year-end recital. May was six months away, a month earlier than her usual recital time. With the wedding, the honeymoon, *and* moving to Portland clustered in the first two weeks of June, she needed an early start. So many changes crowded the next few months, changes that would totally uproot her present life. She'd miss having her mom to herself, but Robert obviously loved her. He would never replace her father, but she knew he would care for her mom as her friend and husband, just as her own dad had.

She glanced at the time when the phone rang. Eight-thirty. Had to be Steve or Lynne. The dancers' parents knew to call her during the day, and her mom seldom called since they spent their days together in the dance studio.

Hearing the panic in Lynne's voice made her sit up and ask, "What's wrong? Is it your dad?"

"No. Mostly my mother. You'll not believe the letter she sent to me. I…I'm sorry I'm dumping this on you." Lynne's mirthless laugh heightened her concern. "This is not a friendly way to begin a conversation. Let me start again. Hi, Marta, this is Lynne. How are you?"

"Fine. Tell me what's happened."

Lynne told her about the letter. "I can't believe Leo lied to his sister and made me the villain. He left *me*. He took the car and our money and drove off. I hitchhiked from Portugal back to Paris—which was a terrifying experience—while he cruised down the road to meet his posh friends. My mom *actually* believed him!"

Marta could hear the tears in her best friend's voice. "Are you going to call her and explain what happened?"

The silence on the other end of line told her everything: Lynne was too hurt and too stubborn to take the first step.

"Lynne?"

"I can't call her now. Maybe never. She's made her views clear, and I know she wouldn't believe me." Another pause. "Okay, I'm done venting. Let's change the subject. Tell me something fun. How are your wedding plans coming along? Have you made any decisions with Steve?"

"I wish I could say I had, but I feel shut out of his life right now. He's involved in a big hush-hush investigation that's taking all his time. I still plan to move to Portland this spring to look for a studio space and settle my things into his house. I'll let you know once I can pin him down."

"Don't sound so sad. You know Steve loves you. The details will fall into place soon. I'm so glad you're about to become Mrs. Steve Mason. It certainly took you long enough to realize how you felt."

"What about you and Noel? How's his kids camp progressing?"

"It's on schedule. He'll begin the construction very soon. He's excited to create it as a tribute to his mother. She'd have been proud of him."

"Is Damien happy to have you back?"

"I don't know. He's so focused on taking over from Madame Cosper that all he sees are my mistakes and when I'm late."

"Give him time. Madame was so restrictive in her thinking. I know he'll bring fresh ideas to the company."

The phone line hummed with silence.

Finally, Lynne sighed. "I feel so out of control."

Marta laughed. "So do I. Our lives were so simple when all we did was dance. My meeting Steve and your meeting Noel changed every-thing—I think for the better."

"I agree. I hope all the changes won't disrupt our friendship. I never want us to become estranged like I feel happening with my family."

"Lynne, we'll always be dance sisters."

"True." Silence once again filled several moments after her half-hearted response. "I know you're busy. I should let you go. Thanks for listening."

"Any time. Think about calling your mom."

"Maybe. Night, Marta."

Marta sat staring at the phone, then got up and took out a photo album from their days of dancing together. She and Lynne, like other *corps de ballet* members, stood in the back for official photos. *Maybe one day Lynne will make the front row as a soloist.*

She ran her hand over Bartley's smile. It radiated even from the back row. They'd had a shaky beginning as friends. Then, after they roomed together on the Nutcracker tour, they'd become fast friends—the three dancing musketeers, inseparable except when it came to diet pills. That had been Bartley's downfall. Who'd have thought Lynne's nagging would help saved her own life? Too bad it didn't save Bartley.

Marta looked at the photos of herself in costume, standing with Steve after her final Nutcracker performance in Billings. Their relationship had ranged from tender to tumultuous, from cozy to confusing. Now her love of him overpowered all the earlier feelings that had kept her off balance. Would any of those changes have occurred if she hadn't moved? Doubtful. *I don't think I could have stood by—maybe work-*

ing as a shop girl—and watched Lynne dance. She doesn't realize how lucky she is, even if she is at odds with her mom.

Hardly believing the big changes that had already altered their lives, she knew more were coming for both of them. *I know we've been there for each other through thick and thin, but our getting married may change that somehow. I still want us to be there for each other whenever we're needed. I want to make sure we're always best friends.*

Marta jumped when the phone interrupted her reverie. *Lynne must have forgotten to tell her something.*

When she picked up the receiver, it wasn't her best friend. "How's my favorite dancer tonight?" She smiled and curled up, placing the phone against her shoulder. "Hi. How's life in Portland?"

"Empty without you. I wish you were here. My little house is too quiet."

"It's not long now. I'm planning the recital and…"

"Marta, have I told you how much I love you?"

"Yes, a million times. I love you, too, Steve. Are you coming up this weekend?"

"That's why I'm calling. I'm going on assignment and will be out of touch for at least a week, maybe longer."

"Where will you be?"

"I'm not at liberty to say."

"Sounds like you're a spy. Have you been watching conspiracy movies again?" His strained laugh caught her off guard. *What's going on?*

"I wanted you to know I might not be able to call, and I don't want you to worry."

She sat up straight. Her chest ached with worry at the tightness in his voice. "Thanks for letting me know. I, ah—"

"It's hard to talk about nothing isn't it? So let's talk about your move to Portland. Since I'll be gone for a bit, I guess we can't look for a new studio for you until I get back, whenever that is. I'm sorry."

"It's okay. You have a job to do. Maybe your real estate friend can look around. I'll mail her my space requirements."

"Sounds good. Marta…I love you, and I'll miss you. I'll call or write when I can."

Call or Write? That sounds like more than a few days away. What sort of assignment is he taking on? "I love you too. Be careful and call me whenever you can."

"Night, sweetheart. Love always."

"Night." Marta set the receiver down gently and wiped aside the tears sliding down her face. Now she'd have both Lynne and Steve to worry about, as well as an ever-growing pile of decisions resting on her strong but reluctant shoulders.

6

Bremerton, November

Dear Lynne,   *November 20*

Thinking of you as Nutcracker season begins, remembering our first tour with Bartley, squished into a tiny room. I think that brought us together as life-long friends. I miss her every day.

Steve is away and can't often contact me. I feel lonely, knowing I can't reach him so I'm focusing on what I can control, little as that seems to be.

I've contacted Steve's real estate friend, Wanda West. She's looking for a studio space. If that fails, I'll need to consider teaching for an established studio, but that feels like a giant step backward. I don't think I can do that.

Mom and I have a standing date for Sunday matinees and tea afterward at Wallace's. It gives us a chance to get caught up. We're sticking to musicals to lighten my thinking.

Hoping you've spoken to your mother and the wounds are healing. Family is important. My mom is often my lifeline and my best friend, after you.

Enjoy touring! Stay in touch.

Love, Marta

Marta dropped the envelope into the box outside the post office on her way to her monthly movie date with her mom. She hoped her comments might ease Lynne's frustration, but only time would tell. With rehearsals for the *Nutcracker* tour well underway, she doubted Lynne had much time for anything beyond eating, sleeping, and traveling. Hopefully, she'd earn a great solo and not get stuck being Mother Ginger, a thankless yet crowd-pleasing part where children hid beneath the dancer's voluminous skirt while she walked on stilts.

The movie, too much like her real life, made her squirm. Afterward, when she and her mom shared a pot of tea, she kept their conversations on the upcoming changes for the Bremerton dance studio: Who would ultimately buy or lease it? Would their changes result in families leaving or more coming? What about Portland? The thought of stepping back to become a hired teacher with no part of any profits was definitely her last resort.

Mom always allowed her lots of time to speculate before offering her opinion. Today was no different. She listened attentively while Marta shared her ideas before she spoke.

"What if Steve takes a job with a different paper in a different state? If you bought your dance studio, that could make a move difficult. Have you considered leasing a space? It's definitely cheaper, at least in the short run. I'm wondering if you'd be content as a paid employee with little say in the creative part of working with young dancers?"

"That's what's racing around in my brain. Steve and I need to have a discussion once he's back from his assignment. We both want to pursue our careers and start a family one day. It's a lot to think about."

"You two will figure it out. Now, let's nail down the holiday groups going to the Navy hospital next month. I think we can provide enough dancers for two or three days."

After hours at the studio, Marta played her favorite classical music as she put away records and tapes and moved into the waiting area to collect clothing and shoes left behind. She stopped to stare at the photos hanging above the benches. She, Lynne, and Bartley were smiling in different professional photos taken by the ballet company. Being one of the three dance musketeers brought back memories of their innocence and their hard work. Madame never made their time in the *corps de ballet* easy. In fact, she never encouraged or supported them. Damien was the one who'd made dancing days tolerable. Hopefully, for Lynne's sake, he was proving to be a better director than Madame.

Thinking about the hard-nosed artistic director made her sad. Visiting Madame, seeing her confined to a wheelchair and hanging onto her anger, troubled Marta. Much as she missed the ballet company, she didn't miss Anna Cosper. Madame would probably wear her unhappiness as a lead weight until she died.

Her Monday meeting with Kersten Grainger, her assistant, began as soon as the day's classes ended. The advisability of adding a competitive dance instructor immediately or waiting until Marta moved to Portland topped the agenda. Kersten wanted to proceed as quickly as possible; Marta hoped she'd wait. Making a huge change so close to her leaving felt forced, too rushed.

Marta watched Kersten move around the reception area. She hadn't gotten used to being the boss of someone ten years her senior, but it still was her studio. On the other hand, having Kersten teaching there had proved a godsend. She'd come from dancing in Salt Lake City; after her marriage to a Navy officer, they'd been reassigned to Bremerton when her husband received his permanent change of station orders would most likely be there at least two to four years. For the present, however, Marta remained in charge. She frowned. *I need to keep my goals clearly in front of me through my final recital in May.*

Kersten took a seat across from her with a clipboard on her lap. For a few moments, Marta didn't say anything. Much as they got along, she watched their differences in teaching technique become more apparent each week. She ran formal classes, a throwback to her own training. Kersten's more laid-back approach reflected the physical nature of her gymnastics, tap, and baton background. When she took over, she'd probably run classes more leisurely, but that would be her prerogative.

Marta wiped the pensive frown off her face and started the conversation. "I know you have lots of plans when you take over after I leave, so I want us to plan our transition as soon as possible. I'm hoping you'll hold off on adding a competitive dance teacher until after our recital in May."

"Why's that? She'd have classes upstairs. It won't be a disturbance to the classes we already teach."

"But it will. Perhaps the entryway can be reorganized before she begins. It's already crowded without adding up to twenty more students."

"We could get rid of your mother's desk. If we empty the small storage room behind her and push it in there, we'd gain a lot of space."

"You want my mother to sit in an oversized closet? Do you realize how important she is to the smooth functioning of the studio?"

"Don't get all excited, Marta; it's just an idea. Besides, you mom is retiring when you leave, right?"

"Which is not the point. The receptionist needs to take payments, hand out purchased clothes and shoes, answer the phones, and get messages to us. Maybe we can find another way to keep from overcrowding the seating area without shoving her into an area where she will feel unimportant to the operation of the studio and can be easily overlooked by the dancers and their parents."

Kersten tapped her pencil against her teeth, drew a quick sketch, and handed it to Marta. "How about we have her students go directly upstairs when they enter? If we add a short wall next to the current observation area, we could add seating for students to change for classes."

"That's a great idea." Marta nodded. "What about adding a bathroom upstairs if the building can handle it? That would eliminate a lot of running up and down, which would be a distraction to both upstairs and downstairs classes."

"All the more reason to get Bev started ASAP. Her rent will help pay for any changes."

"Hmm. That's a workable idea. Let's get some figures on cost." Marta hesitated before bringing up her biggest request. "You know the four women from my exercise class, right?"

"Of course: Lily Rose, Frann, Trixie, and Irene. They almost live here. Why do you mention them?"

"They've volunteered to handle the reception area for free during the first six months after I leave."

"Oh?" Kersten scowled. "Why would they do that?"

"Since you're leasing the building from me for the first six months, they're doing it as a favor to me. It will give you time to find someone who can handle the reception, pay the bills, order supplies, do quarterly taxes as well as prepare and file yearly income taxes, and other jobs my mom does. The four women I'm suggesting possess all those skills. Plus, you'd get all their expertise for free.

Kersten smirked. "Four of them, every day? So, they'll be your spies?

"No." Marta sighed. "Only one woman will be in each day. They're offering to do it to help *you* as well as me. The only things they'll do for me is send me your lease payments. Next January, you and I will renegotiate the lease, or perhaps you can buy the building, providing your husband's permanent change orders don't change. It's up to you."

"Do I have to have them here nosing around?"

"Believe me, you will be glad for them taking charge of so many responsibilities. It will free you to be creative, teach your classes, and still have a life with your husband."

Kersten nodded. "When you put it that way, I can agree to your friends running the office. But, if they start interfering in my classes or become busybodies, you and I will need to rethink the arrangement."

"Fair enough. I want this to work out for *both* of us, Kersten. Let's keep meeting each Monday until I move. Next week, please bring your musical selections for the recital. We'll want our music to coordinate, relate to our theme, and provide for the way we arrange our dancer numbers."

Marta watched Kersten leave without a backward glance or an offer to help clean up the studio. That would be a conversation for another day. Kersten probably meant well, but the leasing could go so wrong if she didn't see the small tasks that needed to be done every day. For now, she'd cut Kersten some slack and stay long enough to clean her areas and grab her coat before her drive home.

Her mind churned as she started her car. *If she's smart, Kersten will appreciate the four women helping her get through the nitty-gritty of the first six months.*

❧

The evening temperature remained mild enough for Marta to take her cup of tea across Corbett Drive to sit on a beached log. An unexpected surge of nostalgia washed over her as she watched the light from the harvest moon dance in the waves of the bay. How many more chances would she have to enjoy this peaceful scene before winter rains and a flurry of snow ended her solitude by the bay? Once spring arrived, she'd be deep into planning the recital and her wedding. Serene moments like this to renew her spirit would be nonexistent.

In Portland, the hustle bustle of the city would replace the tranquility she loved, but she'd be with Steve. That hundred-and-seventy-mile journey would make a home with him better than anything she could imagine. It would also change her life forever.

Closing her eyes, she listened to the gentle lapping of the waves and let thoughts of Steve wrap themselves around her. *I hope you are safe, wherever you are.*

Billings, November

*T*he daily routine of *Nutcracker* rehearsals helped Lynne push aside the message from her mother in the letter impaled on the dartboard. *Do I care if Faith or the others read it? Not really. Except for Carol. Should I take it down? Nah.*

"Lynne? Lynne?" Damien stood in front of her waiting for her to respond.

"Yes?"

Damien shook his head. "Get your head back to rehearsals. Are the dance academy kids ready with their parts for our local productions?"

"Yes. I think you will be pleased to see their enthusiasm."

"We only have this week to practice with them. Touring begins next Monday." He turned to the others in the room. "Who wants to help Lynne finalize the selection of dancers?"

No hands went up.

Lynne stared at her fellow *corps* dancers in disbelief. No one wanted to help the kids? No one saw how it would lift them up, increase Damien's appraisal of their devotion to the company? Or did they not want to work with her? The latter might be a problem she'd need to remedy.

Damien scanned the dancers and pointed. "Violet. Go with Lynne.

You'll be expected to be there from three-thirty to seven-thirty, Tuesday through Saturday. See me later if you have questions."

An audible sigh floated around the practice room as rehearsals resumed.

Violet stared at Lynne as if cartoon question marks hung over her head. Lynne smiled and mouthed. "It will be fun."

Violet shrugged and turned her attention back to the choreography of "Waltz of the Flowers".

The opportunity to work once again with the young dancers re-energized Lynne's rehearsing and lifted away the last of her concern over the dartboard letter. She'd lunch with Violet and explain their roles. If she could get the girl more involved in the company, maybe Suzette wouldn't have the chance to poison her with lies and unprofessional actions.

Lynne ordered the cheapest item on the menu at The Dude Ranch: a bowl of soup. Crackers came free on the side of the plate. Her November funds were down to two dollars and twelve cents after she bought basic groceries and a suitcase for touring. Leo still had her two bags with him. Getting her brakes fixed and the desperately needed winter tires for her Rambler would have to wait until another payday.

Violet set her menu aside after ordering a large salad with a buttermilk roll and a chocolate shake. "So, what do we do with the dance academy kids?"

"Their teachers and I have taught them their roles. You and I will help them practice. It'll be fun. I did it on my own last year, but two of us doing it will work a lot better. Students who perform receive a huge discount on classes for winter term."

"This seriously cuts into my free time."

"Believe me, Damien will notice your extra effort and involvement. We're paid a few dollars, but that isn't as important as showing you are invested in dancing here."

"Suzette says it's a waste of time."

Lynne briefly closed her eyes and took a deep breath before speaking. "Suzette sees the ballet company differently than most of us. Be cautious."

"She said you'd say that."

"What?"

"Suzette says you're a dance snob since you came back from France. She says you only got the chance to go on the tour because you're always buttering up Damien. She says Madame hated you, and Damien wants to fire you."

Momentarily biting her lip to squelch the answer she wanted to give, Lynne spoke softly and slowly. "She and I have different views. I like working with the young dancers. If you don't want to join me, tell Damien today so he can appoint someone else.

"Won't he be mad?"

"Disappointed, not mad. But if you stay on to help the kids, he'll see you're serious about supporting the company. It's your choice."

The rest of their lunch break they spent time talking about their families, their past dance experiences, and their boyfriends. Lynne struggled but kept the conversation away from bashing Suzette's attitude and her misleading tales being spewed to the new dancers.

When they returned to rehearsals, Violet immediately huddled with Suzette. From Suzette's sneer, it appeared Violet was planning to help the young dancers. She'd know for sure at three-fifteen when they'd head to the academy.

Lynne rode the bike home slowly, wishing she had the money to keep gas in her Rambler. After her next payday, her money situation would return to near normal, whatever that was. Pedaling did offer an advantage that driving didn't; it gave her an excellent chance to go back over her day. The dance academy rehearsal sessions went well. Carmen, Lucy, and Tracy's progress impressed her. By the time they reached their mid-teens, one or more of them might become *corps de ballet* dancers for the company. She hoped she'd be around to see if that happened.

Violet reluctantly agreed to be the practice Mother Ginger until the stilts appeared, leaving Lynne to take on the task. Fervently hoping an enterprising first-year dancer would step forward, Lynne frowned. *We really need someone dedicated like Marta had been to recreate the Mother Ginger role. Please, please, don't let the role fall to me. Ha, ha… I probably would fall!*

Other than that refusal, Violet was a great helper. The children were fascinated by her long, bright red hair and her freckles. She learned their names quickly and cheerfully led them to their positions on the pretend stage their teacher set up in a spare practice room. She laughed at their jokes but helped keep them focused. Watching her interaction with the youngsters, Lynne realized Violet might be a good fit for Cheryl's French tour, if she had one this coming summer—unless Suzette got her to join her small entourage of dissatisfied dancers.

Similar to the touring days last year, dancers shared rooms in small hotels, practiced and danced on an assortment of stages, and used local children whenever possible to encourage their small-town families and friends to attend performances. Meals were on their own but paid through their daily stipends. Luckily, Suzette and Lynne never shared more than the bus ride as each day became yet another challenge to their bodies and their enthusiasm. Throughout the hectic tour, Violet remained Suzette's constant seatmate and walk-around companion. Lynne couldn't help but wonder if she, too, would become a thorn in her side.

Without fail, each performance drew rave reviews with photo spreads featuring company soloists and local student dancers who participated in the programs. Each after-function opened up to include not only patrons and news media, but also local attendees, the students, and their families. Damien drew praise for his leadership and inclusion of local dancers. The end result: invitations to return next year and whenever other tours might be made available.

Back in Billings, the exhausted dancers had three days to recover amid rehearsals for their fifteen hometown performances running through December twenty-fourth. The only true glitch occurred when the young dancer taking on Mother Ginger, throughout the season, fell off the stilts during a rehearsal and sprained her ankle. Much to Lynne's relief, a first-year guy took on the part, securing his future with the company for years to come. Night after night, his over-the-top performance generated hearty laughter, and enthusiastic applause from the enthralled audience. Lynne reminded herself to compliment him profusely for the originality of his performance and for saving her from the daunting task of becoming Mother Ginger.

Each evening she returned the boarding house felt like a true homecoming. The only person missing was Marta. She'd called her and connected once, learning all was well in Bremerton; but Steve remained away on his hush-hush assignment.

She also called Noel and had seen him after every hometown performance. After *matinées*, they'd meet and share an early dinner. Following evening performances, he took her out for late snacks before driving her home. They'd then spend a quiet hour cuddling in the common room, stealing kisses when they had the room to themselves. She welcomed the quiet time after hectic weeks of rehearsals and performances. The chance to share her day's happenings and hear the latest news about the kids camp and its increasing list of financial donors created a positive ending after a long, hard day of performing.

Christmas Eve ended the *Nutcracker* performances. Lynne and Noel sat watching the common room tree lights flicker and bubble. This was the first night she could totally relax since the touring began. Noel seated beside her made the evening complete.

"Does January slow down for you, or do you jump into new choreography?" he asked.

"It slows, but we're already preparing for our next program that begins later in the month. Why do you ask?"

Noel leaned in and kissed her cheek. "I'm hoping to get some alone time with you to sit by a ranch house fire and discover more about each other."

She laughed. Playfully bumping his shoulder, she lay her head on his chest. "You know plenty about me."

"Never enough, Lynne. Never enough."

Lynne ran her finger along his cheek and grinned. "I remember something very special about you."

"What might that be?"

She took his hand and tied on a red ribbon, attaching his wrist to hers. "Today was your birthday. I'm giving you a present…me, as your girlfriend."

"I like that, but how did you remember my birthday?"

"When you told me your ranch hands teased you and called you No-ell instead of Noel, it stuck with me. Your mom was clever, giving you a Christmas-y name." She pulled on the ribbon, drawing his arm into her lap to hold his hand as she leaned against his shoulder. "Happy Birthday and Merry Christmas."

She felt his breathy kiss on her cheek and sighed. Meeting him was one of the best presents she'd ever received.

She didn't hear him say anything else, but she felt his body shift. Her eyes popped open when he moved to the side and tenderly lowered her head onto a throw cushion. She blinked several times. "Are you leaving?"

"You fell asleep, so I figured you needed your rest. Besides, it's two in the morning. Santa might not like us here when he stops in." He kissed her one last time and stood. "I'll pick you up around three, okay? That should give you time with the boarders. Pack a bag. I'm stealing you away for at least three days." A big grin spread across his face. "The Lynne wing of the ranch house awaits you."

She grinned as she stretched, then stood on tiptoe and lifted her arms around his neck. "I can't wait. Merry Christmas."

⌒◦⌒

After brunch and gift opening with the boarders, Lynne grabbed her things and sat in the common room, waiting for Noel to arrive. Faith left to spend the rest of the day with friends. James and Shorty, deeply engaged in playing *Risk*, the newest boarding house game, seemed oblivious to anyone else's presence; and Carol pouted in her room because Mrs. B bought a game only the men would enjoy.

Intermittently watching the men play, Mrs. B knitted a sweater for her newest grandbaby while she waited to be picked up for a visit with relatives and friends across town. For days, she had talked excitedly to

Lynne about this evening of cards and several rounds of *Life*, another popular new board game.

A sudden rush of gratitude for Marta finding this wonderful boarding house washed over Lynne. New Jersey never felt this comfy or this homey.

Snow held off thus far in December, but frost covered most surfaces on the drive to the ranch. Holiday lights decorated homes, businesses, and even the immense oil refinery tanks. Crisp air and rising humidity hinted at a possible snowstorm before morning, with *Nutcracker* tour and local performances finished for another year, Lynne hoped for the white blanket that would officially welcome winter to Billings.

Despite its huge size, the ranch house remained cozy and warm; gratefully, she wouldn't have to battle the elements to get to the ballet company every day.

Cook's delicious western-style meals and snacks and the serenity of the ranch house's setting away from the noise of passing traffic relaxed her into nodding off every few minutes. Noel smiled and teased her about her drowsiness, but she felt him tenderly cover her with a blanket as sleep overtook her again.

At dusk, they ate dinner by the fire before exchanging gifts. Lynne handed Noel a box. Inside was a note:

> *Noel:*
>
> *Your gift is in my suitcase, which Leo has. I hope he returns it soon. If not, I will owe you.*
>
> *Love, Lynne*

He looked up with a sly smile. "I think I like you owing me. Gives me a major power over you for a while."

"Not so fast, cowboy. I haven't seen anything with my name on it, so maybe you'll owe me."

Noel picked up a huge box from behind the couch, slid it closer to Lynne and smiled.

"Wow! Looks like I'm getting a foldup car or maybe a television?'

"Open it. But be careful."

Lynne unwrapped the box to find another wrapped box and another. After several minutes, she got down to a flat box about two inches high and four inches long. Inside she found a note:

> *Lynne,*
>
> *Your gift is hidden nearby. To find it, carefully follow the clues.*
>
> *Love, Noel*

For the next few minutes, she went from shelves to end tables, following the clues. She looked under pillows on the couch, scanned the furniture in the adjacent dining room, and finally found a note tucked under the edge of the silver pitcher and tray on the walnut buffet. It read: "Find someone who loves you and look in the pocket over his heart."

Lynne squinted and smiled as she stepped close to Noel, who sat on the couch and wore a Cheshire grin. He crossed his arms over his chest and watched her as she leaped onto his lap and tugged at his arms to reach his pocket. She stopped and stared at him when she felt a small box. "Really?"

"Really." He handed the box to her and waited for her reaction.

Lynne slowly opened the box and found a key with a note.

> *Lynne,*
>
> *Since the first day we met, you've had the key to my heart. I love you.*
>
> *Marry me.*

She stood in silence and stared down at Noel.

He rose and put his arms around her. "Please say yes."

Unable to speak, Lynne nodded. Tears flooded her eyes. Noel was what she wanted for every Christmas from this day forward. A kind and caring soul with a gentle nature, he was the most selfless and generous man she had ever met. She melted against him as his arms folded around her.

"I know we need a ring to seal the deal, but I want you to help pick it out. Okay?"

She looked up at him before pressing herself snugly against his chest. His heart pounded against her cheek.

"Yes!"

The rest of her day at the ranch floated along like the large, white flakes tumbling gently to the ground. They called Noel's father and stepmom, who were at their winter refuge in Phoenix. They called Lynne's Aunt Vivian, who wished them the best. She wanted to call Marta but hesitated. Noel had just asked her to be his wife. She didn't want him to think of her as a kid needing to flaunt her newest possession with a friend.

Finally, she couldn't stand it any longer. She made the call.

Marta heard the phone ringing as she unlocked her front door. *It's too late for a casual call. It must be an emergency.*

She dropped her basket of cards and holiday gifts from her students and grabbed the receiver. "Hello?"

"Merry Christmas!"

"Lynne. Is everything all right? Your father didn't have another heart attack, did he?"

"What? No. Sorry to call you so late. I waited until I thought you'd be home. How was your Christmas?"

"Fine. Are you certain everything's okay?"

"More than okay. Noel asked me to marry him."

Marta laughed. "I hope you said yes."

"I did. Even though we've only known each other since May, I know this is right. Did you see Steve yet?"

"He was up for a couple days but had to drive back tonight. It was good to see him. His newspaper assignment keeps him away too much. I haven't been to Portland since fall, which makes finding a studio space difficult, to say the least. Plus, I miss him when I know he's away from home."

"Has he shared what he's working on?"

"Can't. I feel like we're living in a mystery novel. Can you imagine Steve not talking about newspaper business? I'm afraid he'll burst if his assignment remains undercover much longer."

For over half an hour, they got caught up with Lynne's *Nutcracker* tour, the boarding house, and her upcoming life with Noel. They discussed Marta's dance school and her holiday. Lynne's family remained avoided, but they chatted at length about Marta's. Neither mentioned the strain in the other's voice, keeping most of the conversation upbeat.

"How's Madame Cosper?"

Lynne paused before answering. "She's not doing well. Damien changed the rest of the performance season, making it a tribute to her. We'll be doing her favorite ballets, and she'll be the honored guest, if she can make it. I'm not certain she'll come unless she's able to hide her condition. She's more vain than anyone I know, except Leo."

"How is that crazy uncle of yours?"

"No clue. Mom and I haven't written or spoken since she sent that scathing letter about how I let Leo down. I don't think I can ever go back to New Jersey."

"What about your dad? If he gets sick again, will you go home to see him?"

"I don't know."

A long silence hummed across the phone lines.

"Lynne? Are you there?"

"I'm here. I should let you go. Let's try to talk Monday evenings?"

"Sure. Merry Christmas, my Montana dance sister."

Marta had never before heard Lynne swing from total excitement to despair in the time she'd known her. Even through her car accident and injury last year, she'd stayed upbeat and joking. How had her mother's letter pierced her steely façade so deeply?

Over the next three hours Marta busied herself by putting away laundry, cleaning the kitchen, and pacing the floor, waiting for Steve's call that he'd arrived home safely. As she changed into her pajamas the phone rang. She hurriedly answered.

"How's the most beautiful woman I know?"

"What took you so long? I was getting worried."

"Had to stop and take a break. Even though the highway was mostly empty, I needed gas and a few minutes walking around in the fresh air."

"You could have stayed over."

"No. I need to be at the paper in exactly—four hours. Having a big pow-wow first thing in the morning. I'll be happy once I can share what's going on."

"Me too. I miss you already, but get some sleep and call me when you can. I love you."

"I love you too. Can't wait for us to be together permanently. G'night, sweetheart."

Marta settled into her rocking chair and stared into space. *How much longer could this secrecy go on? What if it lasts into June? Will that affect our wedding and delay my moving to Portland? Should I hold off on leaving the Bremerton studio?*

Marta woke up seated in her rocking chair. Her neck ached from sleeping in an awkward angle. It was still dark outside, but a faint light backlit the trees across the road. Dawn would arrive soon. She shivered; she'd forgotten to turn up the heat in her house when she returned from her mother and Robert's home last night.

Thoughts jumbled her brain; new worries made her uneasy. She was glad Lynne and Noel were engaged, but she worried about Lynne's estrangement from her family. *How could parents be so cruel to their only daughter, who was pursuing her dreams with determination? Her own mom always supported and encouraged her, loved her regardless of mistakes she made. Even Bartley's mother supported her once she realized how gifted a dancer she'd become. What would Lynne do when an emergency arose back home in Trenton?*

The week between Christmas and New Year's offered a great opportunity to spend time in her dance studio, cleaning and tidying up before classes resumed. She spent the first morning carrying her laundry basket around, collecting and putting away more 'found' clothing, sorting through records, and hanging the colorful ballet posters Steve gave her for Christmas.

They'd come a long way from their first meeting when she'd just joined the ballet company. He'd been a cute but brash young reporter with a ready smile and unending patience while trying to entice her into going out with him. When she injured herself one winter at his family's cabin, he'd driven her back to Billings and spent days apologizing to her for the broken railing that led to her tumble into hardpacked snow.

She'd remained so indecisive about their relationship at several points she was certain he'd walk away. Thank heavens that hadn't happened.

Marta spent one afternoon during the break with her mother, making plans for the wedding and three receptions. Steve had agreed on a backyard wedding at her mom's, followed by a reception at the dance studio. Flowers would come from Robert's garden, and Mom would arrange for reception finger food and cake to be served.

Next, they'd travel to Billings for a reception with family and friends before heading to Portland for a final small reception with Steve's neighbors and newspaper friends. They'd end the festivities by taking their honeymoon trip down the Oregon coast.

Since she'd be busy planning the wedding in early June, she'd scheduled her last Bremerton recital for the end of May. Closing her studio meant closing her physical closeness to her mom, dance families, and friends she'd made since taking over the dance studio from Miss Holland.

Concerns about how Kersten would take care of her dance students still nagged at her. The youngsters were accustomed to her traditional teaching methods and gentle encouragement. She would definitely need to learn how to tactfully deal with or sidestep inappropriate parent requests.

Then there was the navy hospital fiasco. What had made Kersten bow to pressure from parents and take a gymnastic team to perform at the navy hospital? The nursing staff couldn't get to patients' rooms with gymnasts doing flips and cartwheels in the corridors. Luckily, the head nurse believed Marta when she assured her it was a one-time slip up, not to be repeated.

Daily calls from Steve brought smiles to her heart. He reassured her he'd see her before he left town, whenever that might be. Marta held onto that assurance as she finalized recital plans, ordered costumes, and made copies of their group music selections for parents who wanted them for home use.

This year's theme, Wide World of Dance and Music, was the first step in closing the door on her life in Bremerton. Kersten would handle the specialty class routines for gymnastic, baton, and tap groups, leaving Marta to plan ballet performances. Together, they'd create the finale. With music and costumes chosen, all that remained were simple backdrops to allow easy changes through creative lighting and minimal

props to accent student routines and ballet choreography. Making those decisions ticked off a huge amount from her ever-growing to-do list.

Wednesday, she shopped for ingredients to take to Mom and Robert's New Year's Day party. That afternoon, she made two cherry pies and two salads as her donation to the upcoming festivities.

A knock at her door surprised her. She'd not heard anyone enter her gravel driveway. Brushing her hair aside, she stopped with her hand resting on the doorknob. Through the window in the storm door, she saw Steve standing on her porch, wearing a wide smile and carrying a bag of groceries.

"Hi. This is a nice surprise. Why didn't you call to let me know you were coming?"

He tipped his head and smirked, "Should I leave?"

"No, no. I'm just stunned to see you on my porch, that's all." She stepped aside as he entered the living room. Kissing her as he passed, he set his bag on her dining area table. "New Year's Eve is special. I decided to hop in the car and come see you before…"

"Before what?" She stared at him. Her eyes widened. "You're leaving, aren't you?"

"'Fraid so. In nine days. Thought I'd come see you so I can say a proper good-bye."

Marta grabbed his hands and pulled him to sit on her small couch. "That soon?"

He nodded.

"Another secret assignment?"

"It's supposed to be shorter. In any event, we've got the next few days together. That's good, right?"

Marta nodded. An awkward silence filled her tiny house before she leaned into him and kissed his cheek.

"I'll take whatever I can get."

At eight that next morning, Steve returned to Marta's house from the nearby motel, carrying a thermos of hot chocolate and a warm loaf of bread. Marta added bowls of fresh fruit that they shared at her small dining table as they got caught up talking about their lives while apart.

New Year's Eve Day brought clear skies, a sign their limited time together might allow them to venture out into the brisk weather. After a lazy morning, they made a plan.

Marta grinned. "You haven't seen much of Bremerton, so let's wander. I'll show you my favorite places and—"

"Don't you have classes?" Steve interrupted.

"Not until next week. We have the rest of today, tomorrow, and the weekend. On Monday, I'll cancel my morning exercise classes for the week so we can take short trips. I'll return to teach my afternoon classes. We'll also have the evenings together. Sound okay?"

Steve encircled her waist with his arms and kissed her neck. "You plan our days, and I'll plan our evenings."

Marta squealed and tried to escape his grasp. "Steve, stop kissing me. I can't think."

"Hmm. That sounds promising." He released her but kept hold of

one of her hands. "I'm game. What do you have in mind?"

"I want to take you on as many adventures as possible. Let's start with a drive around town; then we'll go as crazy as the weather will allow."

"Such as?"

Marta laughed. "You'll need to wait and see."

That night, they bundled up and drove to Manchester, where they could look across the water at the fireworks set off along Seattle's waterfront. From that distance, the rockets and flares were silent but impressive. The gathered crowd filled the evening with ohs and ahs as each explosion lit up the sky.

By one-thirty, they were back at Marta's, carrying their fresh cups of hot chocolate across the road to sit on the beached log under a cold but star-filled sky.

"It's so beautiful here. I'll miss it when I move to Portland."

"You're what's beautiful. I love you so much. Here and now, I promise to be with you every New Year's Eve and as many evenings as possible." He snugged their blanket around their bodies and let the silence of the bay and the faint lapping of water take over the conversation.

Snuggling into Steve's closeness, she hadn't realized how alone she'd felt when they'd had so many miles between them. With his new assignment, which he'd said could last several months. *Months? What about our June wedding?* Her breath caught in her throat. Those miles might grow from a hundred to thousands. Forcing that thought out of her mind, she vowed to stay so busy the time would pass quickly.

"Look up to our right. See that wide 'w' of stars?" She pointed at the sky. "It's Cassiopeia, my favorite constellation. She was placed in the sky as a punishment for saying her daughter Andromeda was more beautiful than the sea nymphs. Now, she forever clings to her throne in the northern sky. I see her as a brave woman, so I make my wishes to her strength, hoping she's at peace as much as I am with you here beside me."

Steve stared at the sky, then hugged Marta. "I'll look for her each night I'm away to send you my love."

New Year's Day, they spent the afternoon and early evening eating and watching college football bowl games with Marta's mom, Robert, and their friends. Back at her house, they again spent time by the bay beneath the night sky, bundled in blankets to keep out the biting cold. This time, clouds crept in to cover the stars, a sign of changing weather.

By morning, the clouds had disappeared. When Steve returned, he fixed breakfast, and they discussed their day's destination: Seattle or a trip to the ocean.

"That's no decision at all," Steve said. "I've seen Portland. Seattle can't be that different. I vote we head to the ocean. How long will it take?"

"Since it's over a hundred miles, and since we'll be driving through lots of little towns with twenty-five-mile-an-hour speed limits and we'll be making a few stops, I guess almost three hours."

"Each way?"

"Yep. We'd better get going so we have lots of time on the beach."

Marta prepared a picnic basket of snacks for their drive to her favorite stretch of sand: Copalis Beach. The trip took them through several small towns: McCleary, Elma, Satsop, and Montesano. When they reached Aberdeen, she directed Steve to pull in at a Dairy Queen,

"You brought treats, didn't you?"

"Yes, but family tradition demands we stop for burgers and milk-shakes."

Steve saluted her. "Whatever you say, boss. I'd never think of messing with your family tradition."

After finishing off their meal, they drove on to the coast and turned north to Copalis. Marta pointed ahead. "Drive out onto the beach."

"It's sand; won't we get stuck?'

She suppressed a giggle at his confused expression and patted his arm. "Trust me, future-husband-of-mine. It's safe if we stay on the hard packed sand.

Steve relaxed when he saw a dozen cars lined up on the sand, facing the ocean. People walked along the shoreline in both directions as the distant waves curled then slid across the sand.

"It's low tide. High tide is hours away. Let's park and explore." Marta opened her door, buttoned her warm coat, took off her shoes, and raced toward the water. Her hands flew wildly above her head. "Come on!"

Steve stared at her, locked the car, and walked toward the water, wearing his coat and shoes. By the time he reached Marta, she'd finished wading in the shallows and was running back to him. Her hair blew every which way, but the joy on her face showed she didn't care.

"That was fun! Your turn."

"Pass. The air must be thirty degrees. How cold is the water?"

"A little warmer than thirty, I guess, but probably not a lot. Don't you want to tell your friends you braved the ocean in winter?"

"Nope. I declare you to be the bravest of the brave. Do you want to leave now?"

"Leave? No. Let me put on my shoes so we can walk along the shore. I love to feel the thunder of the waves and watch them slowly cover the beach. Okay?"

For the next hour, they walked, talked, and picked up bits of driftwood and shells before heading back to the car. Steve turned on the heat as Marta poured mugs of hot cocoa. Within minutes, they were warm and cozy, watching the turbulent ocean edge closer and closer.

Reluctantly, at least in her mind, they left the beach and headed south along the main road. "What do you think, Steve? Was it worth the drive?"

"Definitely. But aren't your feet frozen?"

"Sure. That's the whole point. Think about it. The Pacific Ocean reaches across thousands of miles in all directions. We're here together, one tiny spot on the planet. In a few days, you'll be somewhere else on the planet, maybe beside this very ocean. Or maybe someday, the two of us will cross it to another country that shares these waters with us. It's all one big, watery connection."

Steve raised an eyebrow. "I'm not sure how freezing your feet plays into the ocean connecting us, but I'll take your word for it. When did you become a philosopher?"

"I'm not. I just love the ocean. It might in some way make me feel closer to you when we're apart, even if I can't see you."

⚬

After Saturday's long trek to the ocean, they met up Sunday and drove to her mom's for a late lunch. Back at Marta's, they packed up more boxes for Steve to take to his place ahead of her move to Portland. The rest of the day, they shared special memories from their childhood, knowing reality would too soon cut short their precious time together.

Working just half days during the remainder of his visit allowed them to explore local spots and enjoy the closeness she had missed so much. On Monday, they visited Illahee State Park and walked the trails among the gigantic evergreens. Tuesday, she cancelled her afternoon classes, too, and they took the passengers-only boat to Port Orchard, walking through the shops and along the waterfront, waiting for the first showing of *Pillow Talk*, a Doris Day and Rock Hudson romantic comedy at the tiny theater on Bay Street. After the movie, Steve tucked Marta's hand into his pocket along with his as they strolled back to the ferry dock. "Just learned something new about you—or do you always cry in movies?"

Marta smiled and kissed his cheek. "Only romances and movies with happy-sad endings."

He stopped walking and stared at her. "Happy-sad? Is there such a thing?"

"Of course. Those are movies where everything looks like their relationship is going to be successful, but then things change. They misunderstand each other, and it suddenly appears it might fail. That's happy and then sad. Then they solve their problems, so things work out for the best. That makes a happy ending—which also makes me cry."

Steve put his arm around her, drew her against his chest, and let her cry. *I sure hope we'll be strong enough to survive our time apart.* A little shiver traveled up his spine. *I'll work my hardest to get to our happy ending.*

Wednesday, they drove to Seabeck, a small community on the upper shore of the Hood Canal that consisted of a general store, a boat launch, and a closed restaurant. Marta didn't need to explain why they were there; the spectacular view spoke for itself. The mountains across the canal rose from the water in a gradual yet continuous incline of evergreens topped with granite outcroppings and patches of small, permanent snowfields.

They sat close together, watching the waves, the scattering of fishing boats, and the mountains. "This is amazing, Marta. Do you come here often?"

"Not anymore. My dad and I used to fish here. We'd get up before

dawn, load up the car, and rent a small boat. For several hours, we trolled back and forth and over to a small harbor on the other side of the canal with our lines in the water."

"Did you catch many fish?"

Marta laughed. "No. Mostly we sat in the quiet. Sometimes, it was foggy, so the world disappeared; we were the only people left. It was our time to be together. I still feel close to my dad when I come here."

Their last day together, they spent time saying good-bye to her parents before Steve drove her to the dance studio for afternoon classes. Their time in the car passed in silence. Neither knew what to say nor how to handle the upcoming separation.

Steve stopped the car and turned off the engine. He turned to her, but her head was ducked down as if something important was happening to her hands. He waited.

Silence.

"Marta, you need to go inside, and I need to head south."

She nodded.

"I promise to write often."

No reaction.

"You promised you'd write, so I'll hold you to that."

No reaction.

"Honey? I love you. I promise to come back as soon as possible."

She looked up. Tears streamed down her face. Brushing them aside, she reached out to touch Steve's face. "I love you. Call me the minute you get home. Promise."

Steve nodded and kissed her, then opened his door, walked around the car, and opened hers. When she stood, he pulled her close, feeling her body vibrate from her sobs. "Love you, always."

Remaining tight against his chest, she nodded. "Always."

Getting back in the car, he pulled out of the parking area and disappeared around the corner.

She wiped her face and walked inside the dance studio.

10

Billings, January 1960

The new season of performances created an unexpected stir with patrons and the media. To address the reason for the adjusted schedule and offset speculation, Damien wrote articles about Madame Cosper, her creation of the ballet company, and why she chose Billings for its location. The lengthy pieces, located on the bottom of page one, appeared in installments on three consecutive days. Local residents rallied around the company's special one-time program change and began spreading the word. Ticket sales soared, and speculation about the company closing ceased.

As soon as she finished reading the third installment, Lynne called Marta.

"You'll never believe what Damien wrote about Madame and the Intermountain Ballet Company. He shared how she opened the dance studio for her two daughters, who she expected to be her first prima ballerinas. We both know how that worked out. But I'd never heard that she funded the studio's first year from her savings as a premier dancer. That must have encouraged the arts patrons to financially support the founding of the company."

"But, Lynne, she surely had other help. Maybe that's what led her to her secret benefactor, Herbert. Remember him?"

"Oh, yes. Mr. Lovey Dovey stopping in afterhours to see her. We almost got caught accidently eavesdropping on their smoochy talk. That could have ended our careers. After what she told us when we visited her last spring, I guess she had a serious falling out with her daughters. I picked up copies of the papers. I'm cutting out and mailing you all three installments today. Could you come for the tribute—see her one last time?"

"The Bremerton studio is taking up lots of my time. I can't make any promises, but I'll try."

"Do you have time to tell me what's going on with Steve? Is he back yet?"

"Yes, I have time. No, he's not back. I got a letter a couple days ago that told me very little besides he's missing me."

"That's love, for you. He's crazy about you."

"I know, but I could use his help. If he was home, we could scout Portland buildings together."

"If I was closer, I'd go with you. What about your mom?"

"One of us needs to be at the studio. Enough about me. Are you auditioning for a solo?"

"I did, but *Serenade* uses all the dancers together with Patrice performing the major solo. I tried out for two small parts. Suzette got one. Melanie got the other."

"Suzette got one? Really? How did that happen?"

"My ankle is acting up, so I'm going to the trainer for strength exercises. I'm relegated to ballet slippers, but I can dance in *Serenade* with my ankle wrapped. We'll add older students from the ballet academy to increase the number of dancers in the piece. Damien promised a special tribute to Madame, so he's even using young dancers to show a typical ballet class. Should be fun."

"Why is this happening now?"

"Madame's health is failing. She no longer accepts visitors."

In the background, Lynne heard Marta speaking to someone.

"Mom just walked in. She says hello. I need to go. We have business details to work on tonight. Keep me posted. I'll try to make the tribute. Just not sure I can make it happen."

~ ❧ ~

Practices for the tribute to Madame Cosper moved ahead smoothly. By dress rehearsal, expectations grew wildly positive; something special was about to happen. Widely publicized details of the planned event generated a buzz of interest, starting with the dress rehearsal.

Serenade, a company favorite with its blue backlighting behind a gray scrim curtain and stark staging, created a graceful introduction. The simple, glowing pale blue tulle dresses with unadorned bodices created a casual atmosphere. Dancers stood in diagonal lines, moving in quiet uniformity while the small string ensemble played Tchaikovsky's score. Each lift and drop of the melody depicted a welcome breeze, reminiscent of a summer's day.

Patrice and the two other female soloists moved among the lines, being lifted by male dancers and set down as gently as feathers. Patrice carried the performance with grace and her usual attention to detail. Suzette and Melanie moved in unison as secondary soloists winding among the lines of dancers. When the selection ended, the patrons and media stood and applauded for several minutes.

As soon as the dancers exited, Damien walked onto the empty stage and welcomed the inner circle audience and media to the dress rehearsal. He shared little-known details about Madame's life, as well as filmed footage of her performances as a prima ballerina. Soft ohs and ahs from the viewers expressed their gratitude for the exceptional talent she brought to the Intermountain Ballet Company.

Next, dance academy students shared a typical afternoon class at the barre. Young dancers stood in front, older in back, as the director of the academy led them in barre exercises with their familiar piano accompanist seated to one side. After the barre exercises, the older dancers showed center floor work, then a sampling of leaps and turns across the stage.

The current Intermountain dancers had been allowed to sit in the back of the theatre between their dancing, an unorthodox breach of theatre etiquette. Since this was the dress rehearsal of a tribute event, the rules were being ignored.

Company dancers filled the rest of the program with favorite excerpts from Madame's ballets from past seasons. Applause from those in attendance showed excitement about Damien's directing ability, as well as his caring about his mentor. The tribute promised to be a huge success.

Appreciation for the mountain of work Damien had taken on to pay tribute to Madame surged through Lynne. Pangs of guilt for the way she and Marta had talked about the woman made her squirm. A harsh taskmaster who seldom bestowed even small commendations on her company dancers, she was also the most gifted ballerina Lynne had had the privilege of watching through film. Madame's dancing brought to life a sophisticated vision of motion and music that would live long in the hearts and minds of the audience.

Hopefully, she'd realize how her starting the company in the middle of a prairie state provided a marvelous cultural opportunity over many decades and promised to continue for many more. If Marta could see this side of Madame and what she created, she'd be amazed.

Friday morning, the dancers assembled as usual to rehearse and discuss last minute changes. When Damien walked into the practice room, the dancers applauded. He blinked and nodded to the response, paused, then started warmups without missing more than a few beats.

The changes were limited to lighting, stage crew's organization, and removal of the portable barres during the practice lesson scenes. Only then did Damien take a moment to share his thoughts: "Thank you for a wonderful dress rehearsal. Your timing and uniformity were exceptional. I know Madame will be honored by your dancing."

"Will she be there tonight?"

Damien paused. "I hope so, but we'll be filming the evening for her."

Patrice stepped forward and handed Damien a basket filled with cards and gift-size packages of his favorite coffee and snacks. "Thank you for assembling such a unique program and for letting all the members of the academy and company watch with the audience last night. We hope you'll find time to enjoy our cards and these snacks. We know you always have *lots* of free time."

The dancers laughed and applauded.

Damien's nod ended in a smile. "Go! Get out of here! See you at six tonight… and thanks again."

Friday's morning newspaper posted a review of the dress rehearsal that generated sellout crowds for all nine performances. It announced Friday evening as the day Madame was expected to attend.

When the first night's auditorium lights dimmed, the curtain opened to reveal the dancers standing in dim blue light. The violin section began playing as the tribute to Madame Cosper was underway. When Tchaikovsky's "Serenade in C Major" ended and the applause died down, Damien stepped in front of the curtain.

"Welcome, friends of the Intermountain Ballet Company. This season, we are excited to honor the founder of our company, Anna Cosper. When she arrived in Billings almost three decades ago, she had one desire: to create a dance studio to support her two young daughters who were budding ballerinas. Over the years, her studio grew, and her interest shifted to establishing a dance company. With backing from a generous cadre of patrons, her wish became reality. This year we have thirty-two dancers and are enjoying additional success with our Arinna Darnivilla Ballet Academy that works with aspiring young dancers ages five to fifteen.

"You're familiar with our company dancers. Later our dance academy students share a peak at how our classes function. But now, let's look back at Anna's career as a dancer and the early years of the dance studio and ballet company. We hope you will enjoy our tribute to Madame Anna Cosper, our founder and dear friend."

At the end of the photos and film clips, academy dancers of all ages shared their warmups, center work, leaps, and turns. Audience laughs and applause followed them as they exited the stage.

After the completion of the ballet excerpts, Damien introduced Madame, who waved from her spot-lit seat in the front row of the balcony. As two young dancers presented her with a bouquet of roses, the audience stood and turned to applaud toward where she sat.

The evening ended with a reception in the foyer. Audience members mingled with patrons and dancers. Many dropped off cards and gifts for Madame, who'd returned to her convalescent home immediately after the program ended.

Saturday's posting of the tribute to Madame took over the front page below the fold, only pushed off the top by breaking world news. The community had forgiven Damien for making season changes to accommodate Madame's failing health.

Sunday afternoon, Lynne collected her ballet bag and headed in to prepare for the day's double performances. When she opened her locker, she found it empty. Her practice clothes and ballet slippers were missing. *Did I take them home and forget? No, I distinctly remember leaving them on the shelf. So, where are they? I can't dance barefoot.*

Rose frowned but loaned her a pair of ballet slippers.

Make-up done. Hair done. Now for her gown and she'd be ready early.

When she reached for the gown, its name tag hung in the wrong place on the hanger. That was strange. Rose must be mad about something; she had her ways of letting dancers know when they'd caused her a problem. What had she done to annoy the head of the costume department beyond borrow a pair of ballet slippers?

As Lynne stepped into her gown, she noticed the hooks were cut off the back. How had that happened? Rose might be upset with dancers, but she'd never sabotage the costumes she and her crew had diligently sewn and kept in good order. This was most strange.

Rose ran her hand up and down at the back of the gown. "When did this happen?"

"I have no idea. It was fine last evening when I hung it on the rack."

Rose shook her head. "This will take a major repair. I guess you'll need to sit out today's performances. I'll let Damien know."

Lynne returned to the dressing room and plopped down at her mirror. Someone was playing games. What was their purpose? She had no special role. What should she do since she couldn't dance? There would be no need to pick up stray bits of clothing as she had done for Sleeping Beauty. Maybe the stage crew could use a hand with something else.

Suzette walked past her and sneered. "What wrong with you? Too special to dance in a minor role?"

"No. Someone tampered with my gown. Know anything about it?"

Suzette's eyebrows shrank close together. "I couldn't care less about you and your gown."

As it turned out, Lynne had no job, so she stood at the back of the theatre and watched the performance. Watching Carmen, Lucy, and Tracy dance delighted her. They'd grown immensely in their skills. The good start they had received in Mrs. B's basement had obviously served them well.

Tuesday, Damien asked Lynne to meet him in his office during her lunch break.

Neither of them could make any sense of the damage to her gown.

"Have you had problems with any of the dancers lately?"

"No. I've avoided Suzette, and I am only getting to know the two new dancers. They both seem friendly."

"Rose will have your gown repaired for Friday's performance. Let's hope this was a one-time incident."

11

Bremerton, January

Springtime, 1960

Dear Beautiful Marta,

I miss you so-o much and it's only been a short time. Being away from you is worse than the worst argument we had. Do you remember the one about my trying to give you a ring? Or maybe my surprise visit to Bremerton when I saw you with another guy? I hope you can laugh about those and any others you remember cuz I can now that you are my bride-to-be.

I hope you realize by now that I fell in love with you that first day at the ballet company when you tried your best to ditch me. One of my fondest memories was talking with you about ballet slippers. I've never been sure if you caught my not-so-secret innuendo. If not, we'll have to talk about that when I get home.

The work I'm doing is interesting. This world has so many stories. Even though it has taken me away from you, I'm glad to have this chance to be part of something important. That's all I'm *allowed to tell you, except that I love you and miss you and hope to be home soon.*

Love,

Steve XOXO

P.S. Use the return address on my envelope to write to me (often and soon). I'll also write to my parents and hope you share my general comments with them. (Save my love-y comments for yourself.)

Marta watched the news with a vested interest, trying to uncover where in the world Steve might be that was so secret. Chaos and governmental problems spread worldwide, as did sensationalized extreme weather. Early on, he let slip that his paper and others on the west coast were doing the unthinkable: sharing reporters to expand their reach into breaking news stories. That's when she started to worry.

With each new headline she read or heard on the radio or saw on television, she worried that he might be in the midst of unrest somewhere in the world. He always did love a good story and didn't step back from chasing a lead. He'd often insisted, however, his most determined effort centered with his on-going attempt to get her to marry him.

That was mostly true. When she first arrived in Billings, she'd been so focused on ballet and dancing she couldn't see that Steve had fallen desperately in love with her. Thinking about that made her smile. He'd been persistent and spent copious amounts of time and energy trying to make her see how much he cared. *I'm glad I finally believed him. I can't imagine what my life would be not without him in it.*

Unfortunately, patience wasn't an outstanding feature of her personality. She needed to work on trusting that he'd take care of himself and get back soon. They also needed to work together on the details of their wedding and her move to Portland. His knowledge would be invaluable in finding a good location for a dance studio.

Getting mail and talking with Lynne helped her cope. Madame had been dutifully honored. Her influence in Billings would continue long after she had no direct association with the ballet company. How she'd gone from building a studio for two dancing daughters to being alone and disheartened by their choices remained an unanswered question. That didn't really matter anymore. The Intermountain Ballet Company had firmly established itself among patrons of the arts. Damien could now step out from her shadow and move the company in a new, fresher direction.

Lynne was lucky to continue to dance, but Marta worried about her recurring trouble with her ankle. Maybe that would be moot once she married Noel. He had so many plans for his ranch and kids camp that maybe she'd not need to dance to feel valued. Or maybe dance could be somehow incorporated in the special activities for the kids. Knowing Lynne and their shared desires, she knew dance owned their hearts as much as the men they loved.

Letters from Steve arrived every week but told her little about where he was and when he'd be returning. February arrived with northwest drizzle and chilly temperatures. She wrote back, sharing silly stories about her dancers or strange news articles like the Valentine's Day Polar Bear Swim in chilly Sinclair Inlet. Days slowly passed awaiting his return. *If he's gone much longer, I'll need to travel to Portland and look around by myself.*

When the phone rang one evening in late February, she hoped it was Steve. It wasn't.

"Marta, I have sad news." Lynne spoke so softly she could hardly hear her. "Madame Cosper passed away yesterday. Will you come for the memorial?"

"When?"

"A week from Sunday. You can stay with me or maybe at Steve's parents. Can you come?"

"Of course. Let me arrange a few things. How is everyone doing?"

"Damien is working double time. We're in the middle of performances, so he has lots to coordinate without adding the memorial. The dancers that trained with Madame are shaken—probably relieved like I am that Damien is here to keep the company together. I'll call you once I get more details."

Marta sat in her rocking chair and thought back to her early encounters with Madame. Anna Cosper excelled in ballet choreography and music selection, but her social skills left much to be desired. The fact that both her talented daughters stepped far away from dance strongly suggested she'd probably poisoned that relationship as she had with almost everyone she knew. The only ballerina Marta recalled that she had ever said a kind word to or about was Patrice.

The wintry train ride through the Cascades and Rockies calmed the reason for the trip. The snow that blanketed the outside world was a definite signal that trying to drive the Billings or taking a bus would have been a dangerous trek, especially alone. If money weren't so tight, she might have flown. Maybe after she'd settled in Portland, she'd surprise Lynne and fly in for a performance. Sounded posh coming from her usually frugal thoughts.

This visit would be a nice step back in time to her living in the boarding house, seeing Mrs. B, Shorty, and James once again, as well as visiting with ballet company members. She hoped Carol and Suzette would

be easy to avoid.

Lynne met the Saturday evening train and drove her the Mrs. B's, where she received open arm hugs all around. She'd decided to stay with Marta and visit Steve's family as time allowed. To date, they'd not become close, but hopefully that would change as the wedding approached.

Sunday's memorial for Madame Cosper filled the theatre just as it had during the tribute evenings. Local officials spoke of her generosity and how the ballet company contributed to local cultural experiences. Board members shared having worked with her to finance the creation of the company as well as the dance academy. Following them, Patrice, as prima ballerina, spoke for all the dancers before reshowing photos and film clips previously shared at the tribute.

Marta and Lynne watched the mourners arrive and scanned the audience several times. It appeared her daughters either did not attend the service or chose not to step forward and speak.

The Sunday evening performance went on as planned, but with somber undercurrent in both the dancers and the audience. Marta watched the performance wistfully, marveling at their wonderful skills. If only… A twinge of sadness ran through her. No, she couldn't think about that. Her life was full. She loved teaching and counted the months until she became Mrs. Steve Mason. No regrets.

Monday, she and Lynne got up early to have time together before the evening train whisked her back across the mountains to her snug little house. Mrs. B set them up in her rooms off the kitchen, away from the other boarders, allowing them privacy to talk uninterrupted. "I'll be at work all day, so make yourselves comfortable. And Marta, I hope you remember you are always welcome." With a quick hug of both young women, she hurried away to work.

They sat in silence for several minutes, drinking peppermint tea and savoring Mrs. B's banana bread. Then their animated conversations sprang open like a spring flowers in a rush to bloom. They spoke of ballet, of boyfriends turned into romantic interests, of injuries and disappointments, plus the moments that influenced their current lives.

Lynne explained her problem with her parents and her changing relationship with Noel. Marta shared her plans for handing over her dance studio to Kersten, dealing with leaving her hometown, and worries about the responsibilities of being a wife.

"Do you ever think about Bartley?" Marta asked.

"All the time. Madame's memorial brought back Bartley's. I miss her." Lynne reached out to hold Marta's hand. "I have to ask—do you ever use diet pills now?"

Marta shook her head. "When I moved back home, I was so lonely and so sad I used them as an escape. I know it was foolish. I know I disappointed you, and I hated myself. Having both you and Steve urging me to stop angered me, but it also pushed me to quit."

Lynne smiled. "Disappointed me? Much more than that, it scared me. I admire you for breaking the habit. I don't want to lose you. We have too many adventures yet to be experienced, and I don't want to do them without you."

The train engine pulsed as passengers boarded for all points west. Lynne and Marta hugged and wiped away tears. "Come back soon. I'll be in Bremerton before the wedding as promised."

"I'll hold you to that." Marta stepped onto the train and disappeared inside. Lynne waited to leave the platform until she saw her sitting at the window and waving. "Safe travels," she whispered as the train pulled away.

The trip home to Bremerton was bittersweet. Madame, their nemesis, was gone. Damien now had the opportunity to fully incorporate his ideas into the ballet company. Mrs. B remained a favorite person, after Lynne, of course. Next visit, she'd spend time with Steve's family. Maybe he'd be home by then; she looked forward to that. For now, she pulled her coat closed, leaned her head back against the seat, and let herself drift off to sleep as the rocking train moved westward through the darkness.

Tuesday, when she arrived in Tacoma, her mom met her. During the drive home, they talked about her quick visit and Madame's memorial service. When they reached her little house, she found a yellow envelope stuck under her front door. As her mom drove away, she picked it up, opened the door, and sat down to read it.

TELETYPEWRITER EXCHANGE SERVICE (TWX)
FEBRUARY 24 1960 NIGHT LETTER CABLE
MARTA SELBRYTH
 624 CORBETT DRIVE
BREMERTON, WASHINGTON (USA)

DAD VERY SICK. PLEASE HELP MY MOTHER.
LOVE
STEVE MASON (8727)

Marta's insides tightened and quivered as she reread the telegram. Was it too late to call his parents' home? Should she wait until morning? She dialed the operator and placed her call.

12

The train rattled eastward through dark, rain-filled skies, then blowing and drifting snow. Marta slept as best she could, not knowing what the next days held for her or what would be entailed in helping Steve's mother.

Her mom had arranged for Kersten to take over her classes for the next three days. That would fill-in the rest of the week. Marta promised she'd find a way to be home before Monday afternoon's sessions. She also promised to call Lynne and Doris, Steve's mom, to let them know she was on her way. Until she exited the train, however, she would not know who'd meet her or if she was on her own.

This visit would be more difficult than the one she just returned from. Honoring Madame and talking with Damien and her dance company friends filled a longing she had not known she still held deep in her heart. Her time dancing in Billings had been short but magical. Living, breathing, and performing ballets she'd loved since childhood had proven dreams really can come true.

⁓

The platform was empty when Marta stepped off the train. She walked into the station just as Lynne and Noel rushed in from the street.

They grabbed her up into a loving hug and carried her overnight bag to Noel's station wagon.

"I'm so sorry you had to make a second trip, Lynne said. "I've contacted Steve's mother. She's expecting you at the hospital. She sounded relieved that you were coming. Any idea if Steve will get home?"

Marta frowned. "None. Everything is so hush-hush. The fact he sent a telegram tells me he won't get home, unless—unless his dad takes a turn for the absolute worst."

"Mrs. Mason told me the next twenty-four hours are critical for Quentin. He can't have visitors right now, not even his wife. She's determined to stay at the hospital in case he wants her, but maybe you can encourage her to go home and get some rest. She's too shaky to drive, so I left my little Rambler at the hospital for you to drive her back and forth. Call me any time if you want or need backup support. Either Noel or I can be there in minutes."

"Thanks. But Lynne, aren't you busy with rehearsing or prepping?"

"Uh…sort of. We're in the middle of the tribute performances, but Noel is free to help if you need anything."

The two-story hospital windows were dimly lit. They parked and entered through the emergency entrance and took an elevator to the second floor. Mrs. Mason sat in a chair facing the nurses' station. Her usually animated face looked pale; her left hand rested on her purse, which her right hand held with a death grip. When she saw Marta, she stood and rushed toward her. "Thank you for coming. I didn't know Steve would contact you, but I'm so glad you're here. Quentin is resting. I thought I might lose him last night when he became so ill. The ambulance arrived quickly and rushed him to the hospital. I haven't seen him since."

Marta wrapped her arms around Doris, and the woman collapsed against her. Near-silent hiccupping sounds slowed. She stopped crying as they sat down.

Lynne handed Marta the keys to the Rambler. Then she and Noel said their good-byes and quietly left. The waiting area became silent except for hushed conversations at the nurses' station.

Marta held Doris's hand as they talked about what had happened. Quentin hadn't felt well and went to rest after dinner, thinking he had indigestion. When he hadn't gotten up by nine, she went to check on him. He was barely breathing.

"The doctor told me a while ago that, if he survives the next few hours, he may make it." She squeezed Marta's fingers. "Thank you so much for coming, Marta. I don't know how I'd handle this without you here with me."

"Don't you think we should go home and get some sleep? Tomorrow may be a long day."

Doris refused to leave, so they waited overnight in the straight-backed chairs. At dawn the doctor came out to talk with them. "Your husband had a good night. He's in for a long recovery; but, with patience and time, he may get back to some of his old activities. Of course, he'll have to obey doctor's orders and reduce his stress. What does he do for a living?"

"He's the editor-in-chief of the local paper."

The doctor nodded. "I hope he has a good team working for him. He's going to need total rest for several weeks."

"When can I see him?"

"Let's put it off a day. I suggest you go home, get some rest, and come back tomorrow during afternoon visiting hours. I'll call you if there's any change."

Looking around the Mason's guest room, Marta discovered it must have belonged to Steve before he moved to Portland. The dark paneling and heavy curtains created a definite masculine feel. Trophies and an assortment of books filled two mahogany bookcases. Sports posters and a bulletin board with dozens of snapshots hung on the wall above the bookcases. On a closer look, she found most of the bulletin board was dedicated to photos of her alone, her with Steve, and her wearing a variety of dance costumes. Steve denied it, but he was sentimental after all. Despite her exhaustion, she smiled. *I suspected it, but nice to know.*

She opened his closet and stared at the clothes he'd left behind. She took down a sports coat she'd seen him wear last spring, held it to her face, and inhaled the faint scent of his cologne. Tears puddled in her eyes. *Please, please come home soon. I need you; your mother needs you, too.*

Marta slept with one ear attuned to Doris's bedroom down the hall. When gentle snores came from the room, it appeared Steve's mom slept soundly. Only then did she allow herself to relax enough to sleep. Hours later, well into the morning, she heard a rustling downstairs. Dressing quickly, she hurried down the stairs to find Doris.

She stopped in the kitchen doorway. The woman stood staring out the window over the sink, holding a cup. Her hair was uncombed, she wore a bathrobe, and she stood with bare feet on the cold tile floor. The faucet ran wide open. Marta stepped around her and turned off the water.

"Good morning."

Doris looked toward her. "Can we go back to the hospital? I know it's visiting hours now."

"The doctor suggested we come in the afternoon. Why don't you take a warm shower while I fix us a snack and peel some vegetables to make a pot of soup."

"I'm not hungry, but a shower sounds good. I'll just be a few minutes. You're welcome to fix anything you find in the refrigerator or the pantry." She left the kitchen still carrying her cup.

Good news greeted Doris when they arrived at the hospital. Quentin had another good night. He'd been alert all morning, even smiled when the doctor made a light joke, the nurse reported. *If only we could let Steve know…*

At three o'clock, the doctor told Doris she could visit her husband for a few minutes. Marta stepped out of the waiting room to use the public telephone booth in the hospital lobby. Grateful that she kept an abundance of change in her purse, she put in a long-distance call to the *Portland Daily Gazette*. When a receptionist answered, she asked for the managing editor.

"I'm sorry. He isn't available at this time. May I give him a message?"

"This is Steve Mason's fiancée. I need to get word to him about his father's heart attack."

"One moment."

The managing editor came on within seconds. "This is Ben. May I help you?"

Marta explained how Steve's father's condition had improved and asked him to let Steve know. "He'll be anxious about his dad's condition and will want to know the doctor is hopeful he'll recover."

"I'll contact him immediately. Thank you for calling and please give his family my best."

Marta hung up the phone. *That was interesting. Evidently, Steve could be reached in case of an emergency. Was a lonely heart an emer-*

gency? Not on the grand scale of things, perhaps, but I'm aching with loneliness and worry. I'll dash off a letter to him on the train ride home.

She walked back into the waiting room as Doris returned from her brief visit with Quentin. She was smiling as she gave her future daughter-in-law a big hug. "Oh, Marta! He looks ever so much better. His color is good, and he's sounding almost like himself. Any tears you see now are tears of happiness." She nodded. "I think I'm getting my husband back."

Lynne and Marta sat in the common room chatting over a cup of tea and Mrs. B's delicious sugar cookies. It felt like old times as they resumed finishing each other's thoughts as they spoke about their challenges.

"How's everything at the ballet company, really?"

"Damien puts up a good front, but he's stressed about all that has happened, plus this business of someone stealing from our cubbies. Even Suzette has had things taken. I think she's somehow involved, but I can't prove it. Maybe I'll set a trap and see what happens. It's making everyone so nervous. I don't like feeling uneasy about my fellow dancers."

"Any word from Madame's daughters?"

"Not that Damian has shared. I've heard the trust executors have signed over the company to him. I imagine he'll start putting his mark on future seasons."

"Will you be staying on? Will your ankle support you?"

"I hope so in both cases. I don't want to be a three-season-and-out dancer." Covering her mouth with her hands, Lynne closed her eyes and shook her head. "I... that came out wrong. Sorry."

"It's okay. I left after an even shorter time, but I found teaching as enjoyable or even more enjoyable than dancing professionally. I really

want to keep teaching."

Lynne held up her teacup to toast Marta. "Here's to your new dance studio and my wobbly decision about my future."

Assured that Doris would be alright and able to get to and from the hospital and Quentin's future convalescent facility, Marta called her mom and left a message on the answering machine. "Quentin is improving. I'm heading home. Please relay a message to Kersten: I'll return as planned. Please pick me up, also as planned."

Lynne and Noel drove her to the train, hugged their goodbyes, and handed her a boxed dinner from the Dude Ranch Restaurant. "Take care. Call when you get home."

Marta took a seat on the station side of the train and waved until she lost sight of them and the station. She leaned back and let out a deep breath. The buildings of Billings slowly slipped from view. Feeling that Billings was her home base also slipped away. When she and Steve came back for a reception in late June, she'd confirm that observation. Would it feel like a loss or just a fading piece of her life? Now she'd need to think about how she'd fit into the hustle and bustle of Portland—or would she always be a small-town girl? She and Steve shared the same degree of love and caring she saw in Lynne and Noel, but could they sustain it if or when he took assignments away from Portland?

13

*K*ersten's notes detailed that she'd taken great care of teaching the classes, but the studio was a mess of 'found' clothing. Her mother's work desk lay hidden beneath Kersten's pile of personal notes; class dance records and tapes littered the practice room counters. As Marta cleaned up the clutter, she wondered if having her take over the studio was wise. *We need to have a serious talk about keeping the physical space tidy.*

For the moment, she focused on the recital dances, music, and costumes. Luckily, she had the extra leap year day in February to help get everything sorted out. Her broad theme allowed both of them to choose for a wide variety of music and dances; many were already in place. They'd keep the costumes simple with a recurring use of colorful headbands and glittery gloves. All students loved glitz; that should encourage their smiling as they performed.

Her early meeting with Kersten went well, except for her excuse about the messes she'd left behind. "I thought I'd get in before you returned and clean things up. I had a birthday date with my husband and—" She shook her head. "It won't happen again."

"I don't intend to be gone again during the dance year, but it's important that we keep the studio neat and orderly for our students and any visitors who might pop in. Now, let's get our recital music and dances finalized. This is the fun part. I'm hoping this year ends with a happy splash of energy."

⌒~⌒

That evening after a dinner meeting and chat with her mom, Marta sat in her rocking chair and read the latest letter from Steve.

Spring, 1960

Dear Marta,

Thank you so much for helping my mother deal with my dad being in the hospital. I called her, and she was very grateful you came to be with her. I'm glad Dad is recovering faster than expected. However, he does need to step away from running the paper because it's a high-pressure job. I know he'll be anxious about giving up his life's work.

I can hear your wheels turning about my calling her and not you. There was only time for one call that day; I hope you understand. I love you and would like to call you every day, but that's not possible right now.

Marta, I love you more than words can express. The only telegram I want to send to you is the one letting you know I'm on my way back to you. OXOX

Our workdays are long. I don't think I will be back before the end of May, but we can hope I'm wrong. Each day brings more and more interesting news but also more and more sadness that I'm unable to share it with you. Please know I love you and miss you.

I realize my being away places a lot on your shoulders, but I know you can handle anything and everything while we're apart.

Thanks for your letters. I look forward to hearing about whatever daily happenings you care to write about. The simple things we both love, things that are important to us and to our future, keep what I'm doing and why I'm doing this in focus.

Hugs and kisses,
Steve

If her letters to him meant half as much as his did to her, he'd be eagerly awaiting her response. She grabbed a pencil and paper and began to write.

March, 1960

Dear Steve,

Your letter made me smile. I'm glad you spoke with your mother. Yes, at first I felt jealous, but I know it was wonderful that you spoke with her.

She misses you as much as I do. I knew she'd be anxious about your father needing to cut back. I'm sure he'll want you to come home and help at the paper. Is that something you might consider?

Madame Cosper died recently. I know I complained a lot about her, but I also know that under her angry moods, she was a great teacher and a world class ballerina. Damien will now be able to bring new ideas and innovations to the company. It should take off and grow stronger each year.

Lynne sends you her best, as does Noel. His kids camp is coming along on schedule. It's going to be a great place for kids and eventually adults. He wants it to function year-round as soon as possible.

I'm heading to Portland soon to start my move south. Hope you cleaned house before you left town (ha, ha). If you're not back by spring break, I'll start looking for my dance studio. I've definitely decided I can't go back to being a hired instructor. I want to be my own boss (and yours as well, ha, ha).

Why do you put Spring, 1960 on your letters? It's still cold and drizzly weather here. Spring weather is not due to arrive until April. I'm anxious to see flowers bloom and tree buds open; that will mean our wedding is coming soon.

I love you more and more each day, even with you far away. (See, I'm a poet and don't know it.)

Take care of yourself. Look at the stars and think of me thinking of you.

Love, Hugs, and Kisses
Marta (still Selbryth!)

She reread her letter, then made a list of the tasks she needed to do between now and their wedding. Most everything on her list was starred as essential. Even with her mom's help, could she hope to finish it all on time? She pondered for a moment. Steve believed she could handle anything that needed to be done while he was gone; she would not let him down.

During the local school's spring break the first part of April, she'd drive to Portland with boxes to be stored, stay at Steve's house, check out his neighborhood for available buildings, and get to know the area. *Maybe Mom would go with her unless she and Robert had plans. Wouldn't hurt to ask. We could spend time discussing the future of the Bremerton dance studio and mom's plans now that she was retiring. Robert wants them to travel, but what does she want?*

*L*ynne sat in her room, rocking and thinking as the swirling winds of March buffeted the branches that brushed against the boarding house. There had to be a way to flush out who was systematically taking clothing and shoes and now money from dancers' pocketbooks. Once Damien hired a carpenter to enclose the dressing room cubbies and install locks, the culprit would probably give up and remain undetected and unpunished. The thought that someone could get away with the mischievous thievery was unacceptable.

After racking her brain, thinking and discarding various possibilities, she came up with one viable idea: spread a rumor and then hide out to see who took the bait.

Lynne took a worn pair of pointe shoes and carefully stitched on the initials A. M. Then she took them outside and scraped the toes over rough places in the walkway to age them. After rubbing dirt over the initials, she wrapped them in tissue and placed them in an old shoe bag. Tomorrow, she'd place them in her ballet cubby and spin her story, hoping to catch the thief.

Waiting until the practice room filled with dancers, she hurried in out-of-breath and made a point of looking excited. "You guys are *never*

going to believe what my parents sent to me! They went to a fundraiser and bid on a pair of pointe shoes. No one else bid on them so, get this: For ten dollars they picked up a pair of Alicia Markova's pointe shoes. In case you don't know, she was a prima dancer for the Bolshoi Ballet Theatre. Can you believe it? I'm taking them to my safe deposit box on my way home today."

Violet rushed up. "Can we see them? Are they worn or new?"

"Worn. Even her darned toe is worn out. I'll get them out during today's lunch break if anyone wants to see them."

As Damien entered the practice room the dancers scattered to find places at the *barres* for morning warm-ups before the choreography for the *Americana* performances continued. Lynne stood so she could see if anyone left the room during *barre* exercises. No one did. In fact, for the entire practice session, no one left. Maybe her scheme wouldn't work. Or maybe the culprit was waiting to check out the pointe shoes during the lunch break.

At lunchtime. Lynne stood encircled by dancers. She slowly unveiled the shoes and pointed out the initials sewn on each one. "I can't believe this. They must be worth a lot more than ten dollars. I loved seeing her life in a ballet documentary film last year. I wonder how these shoes made it all the way from Russia to New York."

Dancers carefully passed the shoes around and speculated on the journey they'd taken. After Lynne carefully placed them back in the bag and laid it on her cubby shelf, she announced she was heading out to make a phone call and meeting a girlfriend at The Dude Ranch for lunch.

The group disbanded as Lynne rushed into her coat and headed out the door. When the room was empty, she quietly returned and hid behind the laundry cart.

Ten minutes passed, then another fifteen. No one entered the room. Just as Lynne thought her plan hadn't worked, Suzette sauntered into the room. She went to her cubby directly across from Lynne's and turned to face Lynne's space. She looked around then quickly she grabbed the shoe bag and hurried to Violet's cubby, where she set it beside Violet's dance bag before she sauntered out of the dressing room.

Flabbergasted by what she'd just witnessed, she frowned. *What's Suzette's plan?*

When afternoon rehearsals began, Suzette approached Damien, and they disappeared into the hallway. Lynne moved as close to the door as possible and tried to listen.

Suzette stood next to Damien and shook her head, but her voice could be heard from that distance. "I think I know who's been taking peoples clothes and shoes. As I was coming back from lunch, I saw Violet standing at Lynne's cubby. She didn't see me, but I saw her take down the shoe bag and hide it in her cubby."

"What are you talking about?"

Suzette explained what Marta had shared and shook her head. "I befriended Violet. I thought she was going to be a good addition to our company."

"Thank you, Suzette. Head back to class; I'll get to the bottom of this right now." Damien hurried into the studio. "Patrice, take over for me. Violet? May I see you in the hall?"

Violet smiled and followed Damien out of the room. Lynne moved close to the door again.

"Follow me. We need to go into the ladies dressing room and talk."

Violet looked surprised but followed Damien down the hallway and disappeared into the ladies dressing room.

Lynne wanted to follow but didn't dare. Poor Violet was about to learn just how unforgiving Damien could be when it came to the dancers' integrity, but it couldn't be helped. Lynne needed to wait for what she hoped would be Suzette accusing Violet of the thievery.

Damien returned. "Suzette. A moment."

Suzette smiled and followed Damien toward the ladies dressing room. Lynne needed to act fast.

The three stood by Lynne's cubby, deep in a heated conversation. Lynne listened nearby.

"Yes, I saw the shoes, but I have no idea how that bag got into my cubby," Violet said. "Someone is playing tricks, and I don't know why."

"I saw you at Lynne's cubby," Suzette said.

"That's a lie, Damien. I'd never take anything. I don't need to steal things. My parents give me an ample allowance, and I save my salary from the ballet company. I can show you my savings if you want."

Damien rubbed one hand over his face and down his chin. "Both of you get back to rehearsals. I'll see you in my office at the end of the day."

As both dancers walked away, Damien added: "Let's keep this between us for now."

Violet glared at Suzette. "Why are you saying I took the shoes? What have I ever done to make you lie about me?"

Suzette grabbed Violet's arm. "You've been using my friendship to try to get ahead in this company. I helped you with the choreography and shared my recordings with you. What did you do? You lost my records. So why would I cover for you? I saw the bag in your cubby. You stole them. Now, stay away from me. I'm done with you."

Lynne's eyes widened. This could end up a disaster unless she stepped forward and shared what she'd seen and heard. Lynne stayed out of sight until Damien reentered the rehearsal room; then she walked down the hall and outside. A crisp breeze whipped around the corner, sending a chill through her body. What should she do now? She'd not planned ahead, and now… Was it time to talk with Damien, confess about the fake pointe shoe story? Or should she hold off and see what happened next?

Rose Vargas, the costume mistress, rushed toward the dancer entrance with huge bags of fabric. "Some help here please, Lynne."

Lynne grabbed two bags, held the door open, and followed Rose into the costume shop. "Looks like you are getting started on the June celebration."

"Got to start early. What are you doing out of class?"

"I felt overheated. Thought I might faint, so I came outside to cool down."

"Are you okay?"

"I am now. Do you have more bags? Need more help?"

Rose laughed. "Don't you worry about me; just head back to class. Thanks for giving me a hand."

Lynne slipped into the rehearsal and joined the dancers as they finished warmups and moved on to working on the centerpiece of the upcoming performance. Her entering the room caught Damien's attention, but she pretended not to notice as she took her place and focused on the new choreography.

Damien walked among the dancers as he dictated the new steps. When he reached her, he paused. "Are you okay?"

She nodded. "I felt faint, so I stepped outside to cool off." *I don't think he believes me.*

He frowned but moved on.

Rats! Now I'll have to explain—confess might be a better word—before the trickery jeopardizes my career. Why do I keep putting myself in corners?? Have I done that with my family as well?

Lynne shook her head and sighed. She returned her focus to the class, shoving aside her upcoming talk with Damien in a few agonizing minutes.

15

Bremerton, March

Springtime, 1960

Dear Almost-Wife Marta,

I can hardly focus on my job when I look at your photo. You have the most beautiful smile. I love to hear you giggle when I tickle you. Your concerned expression when you worry always touches my heart. Do you know that you drool when you fall asleep in your rocking chair after a hard day at your dance studio? (I can picture your frown as you read this!)

I know it will be hard for you to leave your hometown, especially since you and your mother are so close. I'll look for a great space as soon as I return. Maybe we'll find one in my neighborhood. It's a great area of Portland. I love the little shops, the parks, and the cubby hole cafes. So many cultures and ethnic groups live nearby. And to think, I found the house by accident!

I'm thinking you might want to consider renting a space until we know for sure where we'll make a permanent home. We can look for a studio where you can make modifications to meet your needs. You know best what that means.

Keep your letters coming. It takes me longer to get them than getting my letters to you, so be patient if my replies lag a letter or two behind what you send to me.

        Love, hugs and snuggles,
        Steve (of course!)

        Real spring here

Dear Steve,

Thanks for your letter. It's quiet here, except for plans for my final recital. I get tears in my eyes thinking about leaving. Then I think of you, and I smile because I know everything will work out.

Things are settling with Kersten. She's an excellent dance teacher in her tap, baton, and gymnastics and passing in ballet. I imagine she'll try to hire a ballet instructor soon. She's also talking about inviting a competitive dancer instructor to rent the upstairs space. She promises that will help keep her payments to me on time. We'll see.

She's kind of sloppy about cleaning up. But maybe once mother-hen Marta leaves, she'll figure out how to spiff up the place so it looks professional. My four women friends will manage the office for her for six months. They'll keep tabs on her, so I'll be able to decide how willing I am to sell her the studio. Can you see my sad, pouty face?

Change is hard even knowing you'll be here to support me when I feel blue about leaving Mom and Bremerton. Got to keep looking ahead. Seeing you in person will make all the difference.

Love and sloppy kisses!
Worry Wart Marta

Billings - March

*L*ynne hurried upstairs to Damien's office as rehearsals ended. "I need to speak with you before you talk with anyone else."

"What?"

"It's important. I need to talk with you before you meet with Suz—"

"How do you know about that?" Damien scowled. "This had better be good, or you will be out the door so fast your feet won't touch the ground."

"Please?"

Damien nodded. "Meet me in the costume shop, *now*!"

She scurried after Damien like a delinquent child on a short tether. He held the door open, then closed it and stood with his back against it. "Well?"

"I wanted to catch whoever was stealing things from our cubbies. I pretended I owned a priceless pair of pointe shoes Alicia Markova had worn. I said my parents bought them at an auction for ten dollars."

"That in itself is not even plausible."

"I know, but it worked. I saw Suzette take them from my cubby and put them in Violet's cubby. I think she's been the thief all along. She said she'd lost a scarf when several dancers lost things, but I doubt it."

"Lynne. Faking the shoes was a stupid thing to do. I don't know if I should believe you or not, but in the past you've never lied to me—even when maybe you should have."

Lynne stood motionless, afraid to inhale or exhale.

"Go home. Let me handle this. Don't say a word about it to *anyone*."

"I won't, I promise. Thank you for maybe believing me."

"Good-bye, Lynne."

Instead of going home, Lynne drove up to The Rims and sat looking out across Billings to the mountains stretching from the south to the west. From this vantage point, the world looked calm. Traffic could be seen but not heard; the only sound was her heartbeat pounding in her ears. Was her ploy stupid enough to get her dismissed? Maybe. But the bigger question was what would happen to Suzette and Violet?

On her drive home, she took the really, really long way, stopping at Josephine Lake to walk around the edge of the water and over the berm that led to a small channel of the Yellowstone River. It flowed east, opposite all her future plans. *Billings is as far east as I want to be. I think all the time about my family in Trenton, but I don't want to see them or even call them. Not yet. Maybe never. If they care about me, they can call me. By now, Leo has hopefully straightened out the tale he spun and admitted what he really did. Yeah, fat chance. It will be snowing at the equator before that man ever admits he did anything wrong.*

She walked into the common room and flopped down on the couch. Closing her eyes, she exhaled slowly. Just then, Mrs. B entered the front door with two bags of groceries. Grateful for the distraction, Lynne shoved her encounter with Damien out of her mind and hopped up to help her carry them into the kitchen and unload them.

After several minutes of quiet Mrs. B stopped what she was doing and looked at her. "Is something wrong?"

"Maybe. I'm not sure. I did something that I thought needed to be done, but I'm not sure Damien will agree. I should know in a few days." Lynne backed out of the kitchen and toward the stairs up to her room. "If you don't need any more help, I'll be upstairs or in the basement."

"Let me know if I can do anything for you."

She stayed in her room and skipped dinner to sit and rock, half expecting a call from Damien to say she was no longer welcome at the ballet company. But when ten-thirty came and passed, she began breathing normally and slipped down to the basement to dance and calm herself.

She slid the recording of *Serenade* on, turned the volume low and stood, ready to glide into the music and choreography. Tchaikovsky certainly knew how to create tranquility. His music spoke to her more loudly than any other ballet composer.

As the music ended and she turned to restart the selection, she saw Faith standing to one side, watching her. "I hope you don't mind me watching you dance. With my schedule, I almost always work nights, so I miss out on programs and events I'd like to see and hear."

"No problem. This is one of my favorite dances and composers. He helps me regain my emotional balance. Does that sound strange?"

"No. I could use more emotional balance myself lots of days. I love my job, but it's stressful."

"How are the emergency medical training classes coming?"

"I gave them up. I decided I could only handle emotional *or* physical needs, not both, if I wanted time to experience joy in my life. One good thing came of the classes. I met a sweet man during our breaks. We've been dating about a month."

"Was he in your classes?"

Faith laughed. "No, he's actually a professor of geology. It started when we shared a table during a break. Since then, we've spent time

together, going to movies and on local archeological digs. I love being outside instead of being cooped up so many hours of the day."

Faith and Lynne stayed on the couch until well past midnight, talking about growing up, family, and living in Billings. By the time Lynne went to bed, she quickly fell asleep, not waking until her morning alarm clanged.

Mrs. B came into the kitchen as Lynne finished packing her sack lunch. "How's today starting out for you?"

"Good, I think. Maybe great. If not, I'll be back real soon."

"Will you be staying for breakfast? It's French toast with blueberries and maple syrup."

"Count me in. That's too good to pass up."

When Lynne arrived at the ballet company, the ladies dressing room was a buzz of activity. Nodding as he passed her, a carpenter exited. He stopped and turned. "The doors are operational. Locks and instructions are inside the cubbies."

A dancer's name appeared on a permanent plaque above each now-secure storage space—including her own.

Violet stepped from the bathroom area with her street clothes over her arm and smiled. "Morning! Looks like we have improved cubbies. 'Bout time."

Lynne smiled and nodded as she looked across the bench between her cubby and Suzette's. The door had no name plaque. It appeared Suzette may have finally pushed Damien too far.

Once the dancers were assembled and ready to start their warmups, Damien asked for their attention. "Due to an unfortunate family emergency, Suzette has resigned from the ballet company. Any roles she was scheduled to perform will either be danced by her understudy, or we'll hold open auditions to fill them."

The room remained silent.

Damien looked over the dancers. His gaze lingered on Lynne for an added moment before he nodded to the pianist. Warmups began.

When Lynne arrived back at the boarding house, Noel was sitting in the common room. He stood when she walked in the front door.

She stared at him and smiled as she walked into his open arms. "What are you doing here?"

"I was in town for a meeting and decided to stop in and wait for you to return. Thought maybe we could have dinner together."

Lynne laughed. "Cowboy, you know me well; I'm always hungry. Give me ten minutes to shower and find something decent to wear."

"Wait! Does that mean if I rush you, it will be something indecent?"

Lynne playfully slugged his shoulder as she planted a quick kiss on his cheek and hurried away. Today was turning out to be a great day.

He drove them to a new restaurant in Laurel. The décor, as eclectic as their menu, offered something for everyone, depending on which direction you looked. Autographed celebrity photos, braided lassoes, cowboy spurs, 45 rpm records, bullet-ridden road signs, and posters of local sporting events decorated the upper walls.

Each table had a curved banquette seating area with cowhide print-ed fabric and linen tablecloths. The smells of new leather and starched linens plus the slick feel of the large, glossy menus added to their apparent confusion as to what they wanted as their theme.

Looking around, she grinned. "If you were planning a quiet, romantic evening, this isn't the place, Noel. What drew you to it? It's a far cry from anyplace you've ever taken me before."

"I heard they have the best steaks, burgers, and pasta around. That

makes it worth checking out, right?"

"Right." She turned to continue appraising the multifaceted décor.

The wait staff wore cowboy regalia and rolled the food out on metal food carts while top forty rock-and-roll music filled the room with a steady, pulsing drumbeat.

"Has something happened that we're in such a fancy-shmancy, crazy, noisy restaurant for dinner?"

"What makes you think that? Can't a nice guy take out his ringless fiancé to a crazy place without a motive?"

"Maybe, but not practical you. What's up?"

Noel reached out and took her hand. "I've gotten two new sponsors for the compound. That's enough to expand construction."

"That's wonderful. I knew you'd find support once the word got out."

"Thanks." Noel rubbed his fingers over her knuckles then squeezed her hand. "I'm thinking of calling it the Triple E Camp and Conference Center. What do you think?"

"In tribute your mom?"

"Yes, and my dad. Her name was Emily Elijah; his is Ernest Elijah."

"Sounds like a perfect tribute to your family."

"That's what I thought. Unfortunately, now that work is underway, I'll be hosting donor meetings and dinners, so I might not be able to attend all of your performances."

Lynne stared at Noel, smiled, and shook her head. "I've never expected you to come to *every* performance of *every* ballet. That's way too much for a Montana cowboy."

"But I want to support you."

"Give yourself a break! You already support me. This camp is important. Kids from the area need a summer and maybe a year-round place to explore and learn new skills and try new activities. Adding the conference center does the same for adults. Both are amazing gifts to Billings. Have you thought about designing it so adult groups can rent it out for wilderness experiences, as well as for the training facilities?"

"That's genius! What would it take for me to hire you to help me?"

Lynne tipped her head and smiled as she slid closer to Noel. "A campfire and a few s'mores, plus a kiss or two."

Noel kissed her cheek. "Done. This summer will be busy, but with your helpful additions and ideas, we'll get the camp off to a great start."

Rehearsals went well over the next few days, especially without Suzette's snears and snide remarks. Violet appeared to have had no problems after her confrontation with Damien. It was good to know Suzette's influence had failed; the girl's resilience reminded Lynne of herself after a year of injuries and disappointments that turned to elation when Noel proposed. Somewhere, she'd heard that if one waited long enough, things changed. She vowed to hold tightly to that belief as her life moved forward.

When Lynne entered the boarding house that night, she saw a letter with a return address from Cheryl Merkins. Making herself a cup of tea, she grabbed two of Mrs. B's yummy snickerdoodle cookies and sat down at the kitchen table to open the letter.

American Dance Tours
2963 Logan Place Apt. 218
New York, New York
March 15, 1960

Dear Lynne,

I hope you are happy, dancing with abandon,
and that your tour of Europe with your uncle

went well. I am still getting letters from the dancers and towns we visited. Many want us to return for a second visit, especially that German celebration.

Perhaps you didn't get to see everything you wanted and you'd like to return for a second chance to stay after and tour again? I have secured funding for another year and hope you'll become my assistant. Jean Paul will still handle logistics, but I'd like you to step in and be my right-hand gal; take some of the pressure off my shoulders. You did that so well last summer.

The offer comes with a plane ticket, as well as lodging (You'd not have to share rooms with the dancers), a food allowance, and a stipend. I'd need to meet with you for a week in New York this May and have you in Paris no later than June 12th. Dancers will arrive by June 19th. These dates are firm.

Got questions? Call me collect at the number on the business card I've included. Talk with Damien about getting the time off.

I'll contact him once you agree to join me, which I hope is something you want to do.

Dancingly Yours,
Cheryl

P.S. If you have any suggestions of strong first or second-year dancers, please have them contact me. I trust your instinct to send me someone who would fit into a summer of touring.

Lynne reread the letter two more times. Cheryl had been fun to dance for and work with, but this summer? There was Marta's wedding and Noel's kids camp, both important events she couldn't miss. She'd promised her support for both, so there was no way she could justify flying away for the summer. After longing for more positives in her life after the estrangement from her mother, she could now choose from an amazing whirlwind of possibilities.

arta loved getting more than one letter at a time from Steve, but where was he overseas? If so, why was he there?

Springtime, 1960

Dear Marta Super Woman,

Thank you for helping my mother through Dad's heart attack. She said you were a godsend, just like I knew you'd be.

I imagine you are in the midst of planning your last recital. I'm hoping to be home in time to be there with you and for you. So proud of you and your dance studio.

Our workdays are long. Being away from you is torture, but each day that passes brings me closer to coming home. I miss talking with you and being with you more than you know.

XOXOX,
Steve

P.S. The only future telegram I want to send is to let you know I'm on my way back to you. I love you and miss you. Can't wait to hold you close and never let go.

Springtime, 1960

Dear Marta, Light of My Life,

Thank you for your letter. I'm sorry you have to do so much for the wedding on your own. Have you spoken with my mother lately?

I know she'd be glad to plan and host a reception in Billings. I think we need it because my dad is deeply involved in the community despite his doctor's stern warnings to avoid all activities that put a strain on his heart.

Yes, we can ask guests to not bring gifts. Instead, would it be okay to suggest they donate to their favorite charity or to sponsor a young dancer at the ballet academy in Billings? Run that past my mother. She'll have an idea if it will be well received. OR, maybe people would sponsor a kid for a week at Noel's camp? You decide. I'm good with any of these or other ideas you think are appropriate.

Mom says my dad is getting stronger every day. I hope you and mom talk often. I know she's dealing with a husband who is reluctant about retiring. I promise when I reach retirement age, I'll retire gracefully (at least I hope I will! Maybe you'd better save this to remind me of my almost-promise.)

I should be home in time to help with the wedding and moving. Believe me when I say to plan whatever and however you wish. My only request is that you love me enough to live with me forever.

Love, Steve (who else??)

Marta hadn't called Doris recently. When she looked at her calendar, she saw it had been weeks. That would never do. She'd call her as soon as she wrote a letter to Steve. Then she'd write a note on her schedule to call her at least twice a week. If Steve had been the one hospitalized, she knew his mom would have called almost daily. Hopefully, Quentin would be the last emergency for a long while.

April showers bring May flowers

Dear Steve,

I love you and miss you more every day you're away. I promise to call your mother several times a week until your father is stronger and back home. I know he's anxious to see you and wants to get back to work. Any changes he needs to make will be hard. I remember how hard it was for me to be patient as I recovered. It also takes patience from family and friends, so try to keep that in mind.

I hope you are writing to him. He misses you, and I know he'd probably like a call if that's possible so he can talk shop. I've sent a few cards to him and will continue sending more.

Life is busy here, but I'll start making trips to Portland very soon. Hope you won't mind stumbling over and around boxes for a while. I'll organize my stuff or store things in your garage (??) It's becoming sunny weather, so your car could be outside...right? (please with kisses on top?)

I'll save you a front row seat at my last recital (sniff). Hope to see you sitting there.

Missing you,
Me XOXOXO

$$18$$

Billings, April

*R*ehearsals for *Americana*, the next production in the season, took shape. *Damien's using the bulky tape of An American in Paris Cheryl sent home with me. Thank goodness, Leo didn't drive off with it. For some reason, I carried it in my tote. I'm still wondering whether my large suitcase or bag of gifts and memorabilia will ever reach Billings. Probably not.*

Auditions for this production took on a different format. After the two principal dancers, the ballet consisted of handfuls of brief solos, assuring solos and partner dances for most every member of the *corps de ballet*. Frequent costume and makeup changes gave the various scenes the appearance that the ballet company had two to three times as many dancers as they actually had. Only if the audience read the performers' names listed for each dance would they realize the dancers filled multiple parts.

Lynne loved the upbeat, brassy music of *An American in Paris*. The simple sets with a backdrop of lamp posts behind a handful of round ice cream shoppe tables and an outline of the Eiffel Tower transported the audience to an afternoon in Paris.

For other sequences, the crew backlit the stage with blue and gray lenses as dancers swirled around a bubbling fountain with tinsel water.

They moved on to human statues that stepped down to dance before returning to statues once again. These simple visuals took Lynne back to her time dancing in Europe, an experience that would not be repeated if she honored her friends' needs over her own desires.

One day after rehearsals, Lynne approached Violet, who'd become a loner since Suzette left. Time to step up and check if Violet's attitude had changed.

"How are you liking *An American in Paris?*"

Violet set down her dance bag and scanned Lynne's face with a cautious smile "It's okay. I'd much rather tour the real Paris than dance the production."

"I enjoyed my trip there last summer."

"Suzette said you were Damien's pet and that's how you got the invitation. Is that true?"

Lynne sat down beside Violet. "As I told you earlier this year, I applied, and Damien allowed me to go. It was a lot of work, crazy hours with lots of train rides, but a great experience."

"I like my summer's off. That way I can travel and visit my friends."

"Where are you from?"

Violet shrugged. "My dad worked all over the states, so we moved a lot. I don't have any place I'd consider a hometown." She looked away, then turned back to Lynne. "My parents are divorcing. It's a mess."

Lynne reached out and took Violet's hand. "You should apply to Cheryl's tour group. Damien will want to send at least one dancer. Why not you? I brought back the *An American in Paris* tape and the Khachaturian waltz to the company. Talk with Damien. It's a lot of travel, but it's also a chance to see tons of famous places. You can easily get back for our next season."

Violet tipped her head and nodded. "Maybe I will." She paused.

"Why are you being nice to me? I haven't always been kind to you."

Lynne shrugged, then smiled. "You've changed. You're more energetic, and I appreciate your grace and follow-through. Traveling with Cheryl is a fantastic opportunity. Think about applying. The information is posted on the bulletin board."

Snuggling next to Noel on the couch in Mrs. B's common room, Lynne explained the upcoming program Damien was putting together. "*Americana* includes passages from two markedly different ballets with two distinct moods. Perky, romantic scenes from George Gershwin's *An American in Paris* begin the program. After intermission, excerpts from Aaron Copeland's *Rodeo* change the mood. It's a robust, slightly raunchy ballet set on a ranch in the wild west. Audiences always love it. Bright street clothes of Paris in Act One give way to Act Two's male dancers in jeans, plaid shirts, Stetsons, and cowboy boots, along with women wearing multiple starched petticoats beneath calico dresses. The orchestra clinches the universal popularity of the program by tempting most everyone's toes to tap and hands to clap to the lively music.

"*Rodeo* represents a collaboration of short, show-off solos and small group dances. The middle-grade academy students move in serpentines that weave around company dancers and created circles before quickly moving off stage. They also join in the folk-dance sections, adding their exuberance to that of the company dancers."

She had helped the academy instructors with the groups of young dancers, an experience she enjoyed almost as much as her dancing. Plus, she had the chance to once again connect with Tracy, Lucy, and Carmen, whose growing skills continued to amaze her.

A cowboy himself, Noel expressed great interest in *Rodeo*, "I can't wait to see it!"

"You do understand it's ballet, not square dancing, right?" Lynne cocked her head and looked at him.

He grinned. "But it won't be guys in too-snug tights, right?"

"Right." Stifling a laugh, she nodded.

"We wouldn't want you to miss wearing those flirty petticoats, now would we? Can you borrow them and dance for me privately?"

She put her arm around his neck and pulled him down to kiss her. "Maybe you could convince me if your put your mind to it. Now, let's get back talking about your kids' camp. I only have an hour before I need to head for bed. Tomorrow's dress rehearsal."

Noel described the pathways of the camp and where the dozen platform tents would stand on a rise near the activity center. After summer campers left, construction crews would begin building a dozen half-walled cabins with removable windows to accommodate summer's heat but available to slip in place to keep autumn, winter, and early spring visitors toasty.

A two-story dining hall and office/storage building would be built near the parking area. All building designs blended into the terrain while using the latest construction ideas, a movement on the verge of sweeping the entire country.

In one year's time, the summer camp would evolve into an all-season camp and business or conference retreat, thanks to the generosity of Noel's financial backers. Numerous community support groups joined in, planning programs on nature, local history, and team building. Lynne watched Noel's pride grow as his vision moved closer to reality. Even more exciting, it was now her reality, as well.

"Your dining hall needs a name. What are you thinking?"

Noel tilted his head and stared out the window into the darkness. He smiled. "How about Moonrise Center. We can brand the entire camp with names to honor local settlers and historical figures. Since the road into the camp will keep it distinct from the ranch, we can ensure our non-profit status."

"I like it. And…I like you, cowboy."

"One more thing…I've been reading a lot of information about how our lifestyles affect the land, the environment we live in. Living on a ranch all my life has made me aware of my surroundings. I used to help my mom plant a garden every spring. She explained to me which plants do well close together and which ones need some space apart. At the time, I listened, but I never gardened the way she did.

"Then, when I was in college, I read *Walden* by Harry David Thoreau. Recently, I read it again. Something in his words speak to me. I think the environment will become a big issue because we aren't being good stewards of the land. Even our lakes and waterways are being taken for granted, as though they will continue to serve us no matter how much we neglect or pollute them.

"I want our campsite and retreat to honor the land. I want us to take care of it so it will continue to take care of us. Those who come here should leave with a greater appreciation for the gifts around us."

Lynne brushed away the tears trickling down her cheeks and looked up at him. "Wow! You sure know how to wrap your passion for your project around this girl's heart. I'm definitely onboard, one hundred percent. Can't wait to be a part of it."

⌒⌒

Lynne's once simple existence of becoming a dancer in Billings had grown increasingly more complex during the last few months. Pressures came from all sides: Noel, Cheryl, and Damien, plus Marta. She didn't want or need to add on her family issues; that thought rubbed her raw like an ill-fitting pointe shoe. *Do I still need dance to occupy every mo-*

ment? Not so much. I'm beginning to understand how Marta feels when faced with an avalanche of decisions. Funny how a simple conversation or a letter can distress either or both of us.

Marta's phone rang and rang. Lynne was about to hang up when she picked up the receiver.

"Hello?"

"How's life in Bremerton these days?'

"Hi, Lynne. It's busy. I flip flop from thinking about the recital to moving to Portland to wanting to go look for a studio space, to packing my stuff, and back to the wedding. You're lucky to be focusing on only two things, *your* dancing and *my* wedding."

"Ha, ha. Add in helping Noel with his camp, which has grown into a conference center and Cheryl wanting me to assist with her French tour."

"Tell me all about them. I could use an escape from my lists."

The friends talked together for half an hour, giving Lynne a chance to sneak in the reason she'd called. "By the way, when do you need me to get to Bremerton to help you?"

"By June ninth at the latest. My bridal shower is the next day at the dance studio. I couldn't dissuade Lily Rose from taking over. That means you're off the hook for planning a shower. She'll call you soon to make sure it's okay with you."

"Tell her it's all hers! If she still wants to call, ask her to make it after seven so I'll more than likely be home."

"It's good to hear you call Mrs. B's home. That's how I felt. Walking in her front door always relaxed me. I could become myself instead of Marta the dancer."

"What do you mean?"

"I loved dancing, but I put so much pressure on myself that sometimes I thought I'd shatter into a thousand pieces. Mostly because of Madame's being so critical."

"You hid that well. I knew you were shy, but I had no idea you felt like you were in a pressure cooker."

"Is Damien still easy to work with?"

"Mostly. He's more tense now that Madame's gone, plus he's pushing me to work at the academy this summer. It's a subtle yet consistent nudge. I hope he doesn't let me go, like he did Suzette, but for different reasons, of course."

Lynne checked the clock in the hallway. "We'd better cut this short. I'm going to have a huge long-distance bill if we keep talking."

Their phone connection was silent for several seconds. "I miss you, Lynne. I'm looking forward to having you here in June. Take care. Write if you have time."

The call ended with Lynne confirming her plans. Assisting Cheryl would have been fun, but life wasn't always about having fun. She needed to put on her big girl shoes and be a responsible adult.

⌒~∘~⌒

The next afternoon when Lynne returned to the boarding house, a letter stood prominently against Mrs. B's flowers arrangement on the table in the entry. It was addressed to her and posted with an assortment of colorful stamps. The return address: Poiters, France.

3 Mars 1960

Dear Mlle Meadows,

I am Senna, one dancer you dance with in Poiters.

I much want to come to America to visit. My friend Belle wish to come too. She is also dancer.

We save money all winter and spring to come. My parent buy me a ticket. May we come visit?

If you say yes, we will come Juillet and go home Août. Please we stay with you?

Can you meet us at the plane? We fly to New York.

We are happy to see you and see all of America.

Your friends,

Senna and Belle

Lynne read the letter again. She *had* said the dancers were welcome to visit, but she had no idea any would take her up on her offer. Now what? New York? Obviously, they were excited to come, but New York was over sixteen hundred miles from Billings. How could she get them from their plane and across the country?

Talking with Lynne was worth every penny of the long-distance charges. Since the first day they met at the ballet company, they had been best friends. Marta had never been part of any group; her total focus had been dancing. Lynne showed her the world outside dance and helped her not take herself so seriously. Would their relationship change once she married Steve? A lone tear slid down her cheek. Losing Lynne would hurt like losing a precious sister. She couldn't imagine getting through the days around the wedding preparations without her.

Whether or not Steve would make it back in time, she didn't know. What she *did* know was that Lynne would be there. He'd said he'd be home for Thanksgiving. That hadn't happened. Even when his dad was in the hospital, he'd not been able to come home. What kind of journalistic assignment was so secretive? Where in the world was he that every letter was dated springtime?

Being on her own was harder than she imagined. True, her mom and Robert helped with the packing and moving as needed, but she hoped Steve would be home, to help her make decisions. During spring break in the local schools, she'd not have dance lessons, making it the perfect and only time she could go to Portland to find a suitable building for a dance studio.

She'd need a business loan to pay her leasing fee, the security deposit, remodeling expenses, business license, and whatever other expenses she'd incur. Robert had promised to co-sign for her like he had on the Bremerton studio because a woman could rarely qualify for a business loan without a male relative to guarantee it. Steve made it clear he'd take over the loan as soon as he got home. The ten thousand dollars her dad had left her as a beneficiary on his life insurance policy and what remained in her savings account had been a huge help in securing her first studio, but it was tied up in the Bremerton property. *Too bad I don't have that now. It might make things easier.*

Back in March, when the four women from her initial exercise class invited her to a country club lunch, Marta braced for a bevy of ideas probably about being married. She'd been wrong. The ladies wanted her permission to handle her bridal shower.

"Isn't that the maid of honor's job?" she'd asked them.

They'd greeted her with four wide smiles. "Marta, we love and admire you and want to take this job off your friend Lynne," Frann added. "She's in Montana and has performances. Let us plan your shower."

Irene spoke up. "And a reception at the dance studio. Your mom is on board."

It had been impossible to argue with them when they were so enthusiastic and had already spoken with her mom. "Fine. You're in charge. Now, can we order? I'm starving."

Springtime, 1960

Dear Marta, Heart of my Life Dancer,

I bet you are tired of my always saying Springtime, 1960. It's like the season will never end, but I know it must. Then I'll be home so we can plan the rest of our lives together. Also, writing springtime on each letter reminds me that I'll be home this spring.

There may be opportunities we have not anticipated, so I seriously think you need to rent studio space in Portland. That way maybe we can build your ideal studio in the near future. That would be fun, right?

I heard the song "Lonely Boy" on the radio earlier today. I sure know how he felt. Home soon—I hope!

Hugs and kisses,
Lonely Steve

She added the letter to the others and filed away his latest promise: *home soon.* What did 'soon' even mean anymore? She hoped it meant *before* their wedding day.

Time for a sit on the beach. Shaking her head, she opened the front door and walked across the road to her favorite beached log. The calm water, lapping as it inched above the pebbles onto the sand, soothed her as soon as she sat down. When she was seven, her dad died. She and her uncle walked to the beach at the end of her street to skip stones. Since that time, she'd been drawn to the beach whenever she needed to think.

In land-locked Montana, she'd had to replace the beach with quiet moments on The Rims or at Josephine Lake. Where would she find a quiet place in Portland? Would she still need one after she and Steve began their lives together? Probably. Having alone time remained an important part of who she was; she hoped he'd understand.

Her last few months in Bremerton were flying by. She needed to pack and label boxes in her little rental house, then do the same with non-essential materials at the dance studio. If only someone would buy her dance studio; it would alleviate so much uncertainty. *April Fool! Not going to happen.*

Marta sat down and wrote an upbeat letter to Steve. He'd sounded so sad as a lonely boy. He missed her as much as she missed him.

April 1, 1960

Dear Lonely Boy Steve,

Your letters give me hope that 'soon' is coming very soon.

I'm handling things and have Lynne, my mom, and my four women helping me. Simplicity is my motto these days.

I didn't realize how much stuff I'd accumulated since I moved back to Bremerton. We could be working around boxes for quite a while, except I plan to stow my boxes and out of season clothing in the studio space I rent. That way, I can go through them after we get settled in.

My final recital in Bremerton is bittersweet. Not only am I ending my dance studio, I'm ending living in my hometown near my mom and Robert and leaving my dad's grave behind. At least we can drive back in a few hours. I'm happy about us but sad about moving again. Let's hope Portland proves to be our last move for a long while. I'm anxious to get to know our new hometown.

This coming week I'll be staying in your house (soon to be my house as well). I'll leave a pathway from the front door to the kitchen and the bedroom. Hmm.

I'm meeting with Wanda West while I'm there. She seems to know your neighborhood and nearby communities very well. She has a great name; should be an actress—but I guess as a realtor it works too, especially with a business named Sunshine Realty.

Sometimes it takes me a long time to make a decision. I'm hoping she's as patient as you've been with me. You are worth any wait I need to endure until you return.

Love,

Marta

She kissed the paper, leaving a pink lipstick imprint, folded the letter, and slipped it into her purse to drop in the mailbox tomorrow. With spring break only a few days away, she grabbed a box and set to work packing her photo albums, recipes, books, and memorabilia.

Portland, April

April's spring break brought sunshine instead of showers for the drive to Portland. Robert drove Marta and her mom the hundred and seventy miles in a small rental truck she'd packed with extraneous personal and dance studio belongings she'd need once she located her new studio.

Marta yawned as the passing scenery whizzed by. "Being early birds pays off today. I imagine families starting spring break vacations will soon overcrowd the highway heading south. Lots of dance families are driving to the Disney resort in sunny California. Bet it will be a crowded week."

"I always liked Knott's Berry Farm," Robert said. "The casual paths, the little lake, and the fact that it was actually a berry farm when I was growing up made it fun. I wonder if the Disney resort can draw as many people? I hear it's much larger than Knott's. I guess time will be the judge of that."

Marta's mom turned toward her. "Speaking of being a judge, do you think Kersten is up to running the dance studio on her own?"

"Her heart is in the right place, but she'll need to hire a ballet instructor since her skills are elsewhere."

"Honey, if you're worried, I could stay on."

"Mom, you've been handling things since I first started taking lessons. The four women will be able to manage the office just fine."

Robert chimed in. "Exactly, and Elle, you promised you'd travel with me to work conferences and meetings. Do I detect you going back on your promise?"

"No. I want to be there for you. I just worry about the studio being leased to Kersten because I don't want anything to cause the students to look elsewhere for lessons. Marta has worked so hard to build her reputation. I would feel better if someone were buying it rather than signing a six-month lease."

Marta hugged her mom. "Things will be fine. Let's focus on Portland. I hear Wanda West is quite the realtor."

Steve's house sat in the middle of a block of older homes in the Hawthorne area of Portland. Trees lined the sidewalks, front yard flower beds boasted spring tulips and daffodils while early azalea blossoms brightened the edges of recently manicured lawns. Marta smiled to herself. *Steve must have hired a yard service to handle his lawn while he's out of town. I'm so glad his sense of pride in keeping the property tidy is the same as mine. One more reason he's the perfect husband for me. Now if he could only come home.*

The footprint of the house mirrored Marta's rental home back in Bremerton, but with a second story that held a large master bedroom, a small bathroom and an office or guest bedroom. Sparsely furnished up to this point, the main floor would soon be filled with select pieces she and Steve had long ago decided would make the rented house cozy and which she had brought with her.

Elle and Robert arranged the incoming furniture while Marta unpacked the extra kitchen and family room supplies she'd brought from home, as well as her bedroom set that replaced the cot Steve had been sleeping on. For the next two months back in Bremerton, she'd sleep on the sofa she planned to sell once she ended her lease.

They filled the edges of Steve's tiny garage with boxes of bulky, out-of-season supplies, as well her albums and the dance studio inventory they'd move once she found a studio.

By five o'clock, they'd finished unloading and stowing everything and went in search of a neighborhood diner to eat and relax before the next day's studio search began.

On Tuesday, they met their energetic real estate woman after break-fast at the diner. Wanda West, a forty-something woman with bleached-blonde bouffant hair, sported a bright lavender pantsuit and briefcase to match. She walked up to them as Robert paid for their food, her purple high heels clicking purposely on the tile floor.

"Good morning! Wanda West, Sunshine Realty." She looked directly at Marta and reached out to shake her hand. "How are you this fine April day? Ready to look for a dance studio?"

After introductions, they piled into Wanda's station wagon and be-gan their trek to the ten buildings in Marta's price range. All were within six miles of Steve's house in a mixed-use area of old apartments, shop-ping center businesses, and a few newer clinics and office buildings. The area reminded Marta of Charleston, the Bremerton neighborhood that surrounded her current studio.

Hour after hour, they checked out the configurations of buildings. Each had strong positive features as well as handfuls of problems. The older building rents, she soon learned, were the only ones she could actually afford. Each needed renovation, which meant checks on build-ing codes, remodeling permits, and business licensing before any work could commence. She also had to find out if she could do any of this on her own, or would Robert or Steve have to co-sign for her.

The building that met most of Marta's requirements was four miles from Steve's house. With its monthly rent, thousand-dollar security deposit, business insurance, licensing, and utility deposits, Marta needed considerably more money than she'd anticipated. Thank heavens Robert was with her to step in for Steve. He helped formulate probing questions and, in the end, helped her negotiate her chosen space's monthly rent down to an even two hundred with a six-month contract, plus the ability to rent month-to-month after that time.

She'd share the building with an antique furniture shop instead of an office, where the tenants would have been leery of her music playing all day most weekdays and into after hours. As an added bonus, Wanda assured her the shop owner loved "the arts" as she called them. "He's a patron of most every cultural event in Portland."

Wanda spoke with the owner of the building, who assured Marta the minor changes could be completed so she'd be able to open by August first as long as licensing and other legal requirements were in place. Wanda suggested she advertise open houses and offer free introductory classes to publicize her new studio.

"I'm on the board of the Community Outreach for Greater Portland. We promote new businesses. Our realtor members contribute one month's lease for each new property to advertise their new businesses. Once your contract is signed, I'll write you up as one of our new businesses to patronize. We'll solicit community vouchers you can pass out to new dance families that sign up in July. We'll also post an article and interview you about your studio in the local newspaper. If and when you join our community outreach group, we'll provide additional support. How does that sound?"

"Wonderful. Thank you."

Wanda took them back to her office. With the offer signed, Wanda promised to meet with the owner the next day. The new studio would become a reality very soon. Marta temporarily borrowed money from her mom and Robert until Steve returned. There'd be no turning back.

Along the evening drive back to Bremerton, Marta reflected on her future. Her life would be filled to the brim from now until August but, knowing where she'd hold classes lifted a heavy burden off her shoulders. After the recital, she'd drive down the rest of her belongings and store most everything in the dance studio, out of the way of the remodeling. April was proving to be one of her best months ever.

Back home, Marta, Robert, and her mom mulled over the floor plan of the building. With two well-placed walls, she'd create a second room for small classes and space for a reception area with seating similar to her Bremerton studio. With a long counter installed in each new space, she'd have storage for her records and tapes, boxes of extra supplies, dance clothing, and shoes—all out of sight but within easy reach. She smiled. *Another issue handled.*

That night, she couldn't sleep. Was it the couch or anxiety that kept her awake? Probably both. How long would it *really* take the owner to get permits and make modifications? When should she order two wall-size mirrors, connect phone service, and what should she name her studio? Most every task required an outlay of money, further dwindling her savings and increasing her private loan from her mom and Robert. Maybe she'd not get another full night's sleep until the move was complete.

The next morning, she wrote a letter to Steve, sharing her trip to Portland and the outcome of her search for a studio. He'd be proud of all she'd accomplished. Maybe she was on her way to becoming a responsible adult sooner than she'd anticipated.

21

Four days later, Wanda West left a message on the dance studio phone: "Everything's approved. I've mailed you a copy of the agreement. Plan to come down ASAP with a notarized copy of the contract plus your deposits. I expect the owner to have the walls and counters completed within two weeks of getting the remodel permit. The contract goes into effect the first of June or when the renovations are completed. After that, you're free to paint and move in. Make sure Robert signs the contract and that his signature is notarized."

Marta and her mom listened to the recorded call twice, then checked the dance studio calendar.

"Congrats, Marta. Looks like you'll need to drive down with your paperwork right away. Do you want me to go with you?"

"Yes. I'd love the company. We could take down more boxes and stay in Steve's house overnight." Marta let out a long sigh. "This is really happening, isn't it?"

Her mom smiled. "Yes, it is. I'm so proud of you for taking on this huge change. From the time you were a little girl, I knew you'd be a trailblazer and a capable young woman."

The early morning exercise class members stood outside the studio

entry, laughing and talking when Marta and her mom arrived.

"You two look excited. What's happening?" Irene asked.

"The Portland studio lease is approved. Looks like we'll have the remodel and painting done by June."

"That's wonderful. Can we help in any way?" asked Trixie.

"Not unless you know someone who wants to buy this studio."

Trixie frowned. "I thought Kersten was taking over."

"She is, and she'll be great. It would just have been simpler for Marta if she'd gotten a sale instead of a lease. Knowing you four are handling the office details is a huge relief. Robert and I are ready to spend more time together, especially when his work takes us to the east coast and the southwest."

"Sounds like fun. However, no one will ever be able to replace you, Elle."

Marta nodded. "That's right. Mom's given me super support and so much of her time, and Robert's been very patient. They're long overdue for some significant togetherness."

Elle blushed as Marta unlocked the studio door and let them inside.

Irene sat on the bench to change her shoes. "We're sure going to miss you two. We looked for over a year to find a program that suited us before we found you. The programs we found for women were exaggerations of high school gym classes. The instructors, all men, believe fully grown women can birth babies and do heavy housework, but are too delicate to handle their exercise routines. Gr-r-r-r-r."

"When we were on our agreed-upon last quest to find what we wanted, we stopped at your studio to see if we could use your restroom," Frann said. "One peak at what you were doing with older women who wanted the grace and flexibility of a ballerina but did not aspire being a ballerina, and we knew you were exactly what we were looking for. If

Lilly Rose hadn't had to go, we might never have found you."

Six other women hurried into the room to change. Marta put on the music, and, in a few minutes, all thoughts of the Portland studio took a backseat to leading the women through several stretches similar to those practiced in warmups before ballet lessons and performances. Then they segued into the muscle strengthening routine she had developed to help them tone their bodies, increase energy, and build endurance. The ten-minute cooldown at the end helped their bodies return to pre-exercise levels and eased them back into their day's endeavors.

Marta added another chore to her to-do list; find a suitable instructor for this class. The popular offering had been her mom's brainstorm and opened the door to busy mothers and older women. The outfitting of the small studio as a babysitting room was the final touch, providing supervised activities while the moms enjoyed a workout designed for their needs.

Drives to and from Portland became a weekly trek throughout the rest of April and into May. Each Saturday after classes ended, Marta and her mom drove south. They spent Sundays and Mondays unpacking and stowing things in Steve's house, anticipating the time they'd be able to get into the new studio to paint and stash the boxes.

True to his promise that he'd work quickly, the owner finished the walls and counters sooner than expected, opening up the studio space to their planning and painting in record time. Marta sent Steve a letter about all that had happened. She ended, writing, 'It's almost ours now. This is so exciting!'

All Marta's Bremerton classes were busy adding finishing touches for the upcoming recital. With only three weeks until the performance,

Marta felt a hollowness take over. Her hands shook for no reason. She walked around the classrooms, forgetting what she was looking for or laying down whatever she was carrying, only to pick it up and carry it elsewhere. More and more, her attention waivered while she taught, forcing her to go back over dance movements to ensure she'd shared the changes she truly wanted. Worst of all, she wanted more time to be alone.

With the new studio taking shape, she realized she was grieving about leaving the old one and about leaving Bremerton, her lifetime home. This next step in her life would take her away from the comfort of her hometown and toss her headlong into a large city with traffic, streets to learn, and much more.

So far, she and her mom found most everything they needed close by: groceries, variety stores, a lumber yard, appliance shops, gas stations, clothing shops, theatres, and parks. Everything existed within an easy drive. When Steve returned, they'd venture out, finding other places they'd need or things they'd want. Everything would work out.

Steve's latest letter didn't mention when he'd return. She tired of asking and getting non-specific information. She also tired of following international news, wondering which, if any, of the highlighted places were where he'd been sent. He was a newspaper reporter, not a soldier of fortune or some government agent. Surely, his boss wouldn't have sent him into possible danger.

Her latest conversation with Lynne indicated their *Americana* program enjoyed praise from the ballet patrons. "You would be so proud of the little girls we taught. They are excellent dancers. They send you their best."

"Will you take that summer job at the academy?"

Lynne paused. "Looks that way. Two young dancers from France are coming to visit. They'll temporarily enroll in the academy and be housed with an academy family that has a teenage daughter. Together, we'll keep them entertained."

"How are you getting them from New York to Billings?"

Lynne laughed. "It looked like a huge problem, but it turned out Jean Paul, Cheryl's assistant last year, will meet them in New York. He's offered to take them around the city for a few days, then put them on the train to Billings. Without his help, I'd have had to tell the girls they couldn't come. Knowing a few people outside Billings saved the day."

"That sounds wonderful. Bet you wish Cheryl had asked you to return, maybe as a helper or something."

Lynne hesitated. She wanted to tell Marta the truth, but it would devastate her to know Lynne gave up a trip to France to be with her on her wedding day. She skirted the comment: "I've convinced Violet, one of the new members of the company, to apply for Cheryl's touring group. She's fairly mellow now that Suzette is gone. How Suzette lasted as long as she did is a marvel. Enough about me. How's your new studio coming?"

"Great! I drove down last weekend. The new walls and counters are perfect. I painted both practice rooms a warm honey yellow and the bathroom a light blue. It's starting to look just the way I envisioned it. After the recital, I'll head down with my remaining boxes and dance music since Kersten has her own supplies. Still need a sound system. It's shocking how much money it takes to set up the new studio."

"Ah, but Marta, it will have your touch and in no time be filled with paying customers. Have you thought of a name for the studio?"

"Right now, I'm leaning toward the Dance Elegance Studio or maybe the Portland Dance Academy. What do you think?"

"I like the idea of the academy if your goal is to prep dancers for a career."

"You're right. Maybe I'll keep it simple and call it Portland Dance Studio.

"Sounds perfect. Did I tell you the latest on Noel's project? The kids camp is ready for July campers, and his corporate center will be completed soon. There's surprising interest in taking people out of stuffy offices and challenging them to work outside as teams. Sounds strange to me. I'd think they'd want cushy hotel accommodations with room service, day spas, and swimming pools instead of chuck wagon grub, outdoor courses, and horseback riding. But what do I know? He's happy and so are the groups that have already signed up."

"Fantastic. Steve and I will stop in when we're in Billings for our wedding reception there. I'm inviting you, Noel, Damien, Jer, Patrice, Mrs. B, and the boarders, so I'll know a few people. The rest will be newspaper people and Mason family friends."

"Count us in. Sounds like a great reason for a party."

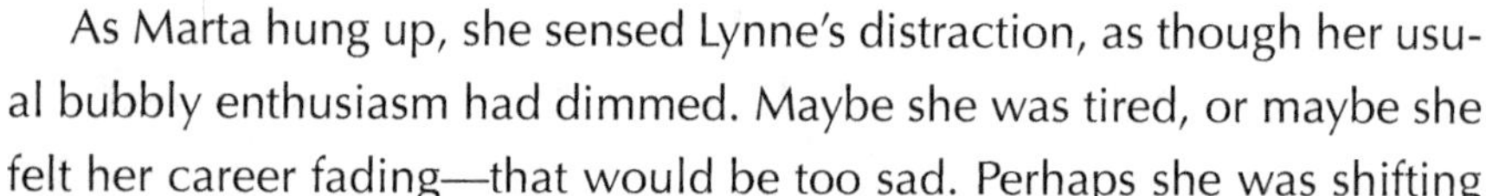

As Marta hung up, she sensed Lynne's distraction, as though her usual bubbly enthusiasm had dimmed. Maybe she was tired, or maybe she felt her career fading—that would be too sad. Perhaps she was shifting her own uncertain future onto Lynne instead keeping it to herself.

After Lynne hung up, she returned to her room and sat in the rocking chair, staring at the large trees outside that would soon wear branches covered with green leaves. Late spring brought back images of the flower beds back home in Trenton. Her father tended each with care, a surprise because otherwise he was an impatient man. Maybe her mother agitated him enough to make him seek escape. She frowned. *Mom's always annoyed with everyone—except her dear boys. I seem to be the one in the family who displeases her the most. It doesn't matter whether she's talking to me or calling me, or writing a letter, she has no patience. I'm so tired of her referring to me as ungrateful. I doubt she'll ever accept that dance is my passion as well as my profession.*

Taking a deep breath, she sighed. Did she know what she wanted, besides being with and supporting Noel? Yes. Deep down she knew she'd continue to dance as much as her ankle allowed. Did that mean she should step back, take the pressure off her ankle, move over to teach full time in the academy, or stick with the ballet company and pray she could dance several more years? It was no contest. Dancing would always win. She closed her eyes and rocked until dinner time.

As usual, Carol ate with her head down, while the rest of the boarders carried on a conversation ranging from James's oil refinery news and Shorty's mining updates to Faith's adventures with her boyfriend, to Mrs. B's opinion on Billings' efforts to move forward into the progressive sixties.

Lynne shared the latest on the *Americana* program. "When Damien added the young dancers from the academy, ticket sales jumped up. He's thrilled that the community enjoys watching Billings' own young ones dancing alongside the professionals."

"I know I like it," James said. "The kids are so earnest in their dancing. Do you think any will become part of the ballet company when they're old enough?"

"That's the goal. Several students who hope to pursue dancing as a career will save money by living at home while receiving excellent training at the academy. For others, dancing is an important way to build self-confidence."

Faith turned to Lynne. "When do dancers feel confident enough in their dancing to audition to become professionals?"

The question startled Lynne. Did she ever really think she was good enough? The boarders, except for Carol stared at her, waiting for an answer. "When I was fourteen, I thought I wanted to dance professionally. But I didn't know if I was strong enough until I went to my first audition in New York City. It was crazy. Must have been a hundred dancers there.

"We divided into groups of twenty. I was so nervous I almost threw up. Sorry. That's not a great dinner topic. When I didn't make the cut, I was devastated, so I worked a lot harder over the next three years. Here I am."

Mrs. B raised her water glass to Lynne. "A toast to your continued success. We're glad you're here."

Everyone except Carol raise a glass. She grumbled something and kept eating.

Americana performances continued to sell out. While the dancers revisited various sections Damien wanted improved, they also started on preparation for the June Showcase, a retrospective of past seasonal favorites, including excerpts from *Coppelia, Swan Lake,* and *Les Sylphides,* as well as from *Nutcracker.* He also added *Prodigal Son* and *Three-Corner Hat,* works he'd performed when he danced in the then-newly-formed Intermountain Ballet Company. These last selections provided an abundance of male solo opportunities, something lacking in past seasons he planned to remedy moving forward.

Four dance academy performances would be inserted before Lynne's favorite, Khachaturian's *Masquerade Waltz,* ended the showcase with a special touch of class.

She'd planned to audition for several different excerpts, but once she told Damien about Marta's wedding on June twelfth and that she was maid of honor, he shook his head.

His jaw tightened and his eyes narrowed. "Not going to happen."

She couldn't believe what he was saying. "Could I be a backup?"

"Definitely not. What if we needed you on June twelfth? You'd be in Bremerton."

She wished the floor would open and she could drop away. "What will you allow me to do?"

Damien paced his office. "As I see it, you are of almost no use to us."

Lynne blinked as tears hovered in her eyes.

"Think about this from my perspective. I can't use you or pay you if you won't be here for the entire length of the Showcase." He opened his office door. "Let me think on this. Come back tomorrow after class."

Lynne slowly backed out of the room, then ran down the stairs, grabbed her street clothes and her dance bag, and exited the building.

Once in her car, she let her tears fall, hoping no one would be around to notice.

Tap, tap, tap.

She ignored whoever was standing beside her car.

Tap, tap, tap.

She angrily wiped her face and rolled down her window, ready to yell at the intrusion.

Jer stared at her. "You okay?"

"No."

"Want to talk?"

"I guess. Let's get away from here. Got time to ride with me to The Rims?"

"Sure." Jer circled the car and hopped in the front seat as Lynne started the engine.

They rode in silence out of town, up the hill toward the airport, and turned right to The Rims Overlook. She turned off the engine and rolled down her window to let the steamed-up windows clear.

Jer turned to face Lynne. "What's going on with you this time?"

She shrugged and tightened her jaw. "Nothing at all. Just Damien writing me out of the Showcase."

"Because of Marta's wedding?"

"Not only that, I won't get paid for June. Right now, I'm not sure if I'm welcome to attend rehearsals. He'll decide tomorrow."

"Can't say I'm surprised. Marta should have known you'd still be under contract."

"She has her reasons for choosing the middle of June. She's my best friend. I can't turn my back on her."

They sat side by side looking out at Billings and the surrounding mountains and plains for several minutes. Lynne felt the tension slide out of her body but remained quiet.

Jer broke the silence. "Let me buy you a Dude Ranch Restaurant burger and a milk shake. I can't think of anything on an empty stomach."

"Not today, but thanks for coming here with me. I know this is what I deserve, but…." She restarted the car. "You need to go home. Your girlfriend is probably wondering where you've gone. I'll drop you off and…"

"I hope this works out. Want me to sing on the drive back to the company parking lot?"

Despite her sadness, Lynne laughed. "No thanks. I've had enough torture for one day."

After dropping Jer off, she drove to Josephine Lake and pulled up near the cattails. Roosting redwing blackbirds hung on their stalks. Life looked so easy for them: sit, grab bugs, sing a song, fly to another cattail, repeat the process.

She scolded herself. Maybe if she'd mentioned Marta's wedding sooner— no—he might have fired her. He still might. She watched ducks paddle around on the lake as she climbed out of her car and walked over the ridge to the river.

The Yellowstone meandered with a deceptive nonchalance. Every year, unsuspecting teens floated the river when it was at flood stage; some drowned. Why did so many situations have such stark outcomes? She should have anticipated her situation and Damien's reaction; she'd need to accept the consequences.

She skipped dinner, but a knock at her door around seven meant Mrs. B had left her a tray. Was she hungry? Not really, but she needed to eat to keep her energy up in case…

The next day's rehearsals dragged on and on and on. Lynne waited until everyone left the dressing room before she walked upstairs to Damien's office and knocked.

He opened the door and nodded for her to enter. "I wondered if you were coming."

Lynne didn't answer.

"Here's the deal. Come for rehearsals. Attend any small classes you wish. Then at three o'clock, go over to the dance academy and work with the young dancers' classes until seven or eight. I will pay you for those hours. What you want to tell the others is up to you. Understand?"

Lynn nodded, forcing herself to meet Damien's eyes while her body vibrated and tears threatened to spill down her cheeks.

"Any questions?"

"Might I help teach the Khachaturian selection I performed in Germany? I know Jer would help if you'd let him."

"I'll think about it. Any more questions?"

Lynne nodded. "May I return to the company next August?"

"Of course. I realize you have no control over Marta's plans, but this will *absolutely* be the last special treatment you'll receive…ever. Understood?"

"Yes. Thank you."

Lynne dashed from the building and hurried to unlock her Rambler. Looking up, she saw Jer leaning against the hood of his car. He gave her a tentative thumbs up.

She returned it and smiled.

He climbed into his car and drove up next to her, handed her a brown paper bag, and drove off.

The bag held a Dude Ranch Restaurant burger and a milkshake.

Lynne laughed, wiped away her tears, and started her car. She'd miss him when he left at the end of the season.

23

With daylight and mild temperatures lasting a little longer each day, Lynne drove out to Noel's ranch to see how the camp was progressing. Thinking she'd find him at the construction site even though it was close to six-thirty, she took the new entrance directly to that area. A roll of plans tucked securely under one arm, he stood on Moonrise Point, staring into the fading sunlight. He turned as her car approached.

His broad smile greeted her. "Hey! Was I expecting you?"

She shook her head. "No. I invited myself. Seems you are too busy to call me these days."

He checked the date on his watch. "I thought you had performances through… Oh, it's May twenty-third. Sorry. How did it go?"

"Fine. How are you? Am I interrupting?"

Noel opened her driver's side door, pulled her to standing, and kissed her forehead. "Everything is perfect now that you're here. Can you stay, have dinner with me?"

"I ate hours ago, but I missed you. So here I am."

Noel took her arm and walked her along the ridge. He pointed to a series of platforms with canvas tent tops. "We're almost done with this part, so the kids camp can begin on time. We expect all forty cots will be filled. We're starting with elementary kids from afterschool daycare. Each will be here a week, free of charge. You should see the list of volunteers offering their skills for the first go-round. Billings has embraced this venture with open arms."

"Hm-m. Maybe you could put one of those arms around me and—" Suddenly Lynne was swept into Noel's arms and smothered with kisses.

"That's more like it, cowboy."

"I'm sorry I've been so busy. Can you stay and talk? Cook made a berry pie earlier today."

"Lead the way. I have room for a piece of pie with a little conversation."

Sitting on the couch next to Noel helped her relax. What was it about him that calmed her? Maybe it was the surroundings, the spaciousness, or the quiet. Whatever it was, she could get used to it in a hurry.

When Lynne looked over, Noel was staring at her. "Where were you just now?"

"Thinking about why I feel so comfortable here with you."

"You mean it's not my arm sliding around you like this?" He moved closer to kiss her forehead as he pulled her against him.

"Well, it is that, but it's also this place—the quiet, the views, the pie."

"The pie? Really?"

Lynne laughed. "You have to admit Cook is a master in the kitchen. You *do* know I can barely burn water."

Noel kissed her forehead again. "I know. But you have other loveable qualities."

"Like what?"

Noel tapped his lips and grinned. "Huh. Can't think of a single thing at the moment." He laughed, then grew serious. "I love you for who you are, not for what you can or can't do. We have Cook. You don't need to hone your culinary skills. Now, how about we set a date?"

"Date for what?"

"For you to marry me. How's this summer or in the fall? We could have a gorgeous wedding in the gazebo. Fall colors make a good backdrop for a celebration."

Her mouth dropped open. "So soon? You hardly know me."

"I know enough. I'll let you set the pace, just don't keep me in agony too much longer."

"Let's wait until after you attend Marta's wedding. All the hubbub may scare you away. You are still going to Bremerton with me, right?"

"I'll try. But back up. You've not mentioned the Showcase. That comes first, right? You've saved me a ticket I hope."

Lynne pulled her lips into a tight pucker. "About that. I won't be performing."

"What? Why not?"

"The program runs until June eighteenth. I need to be in Bremerton by June ninth. Damien made it very clear that since I can't dance for the entire length of the Showcase, I can't participate. I may learn the dances, but he's cut my salary off as of the end of May and—"

"Why haven't you told me about this? Can you afford to travel to Bremerton? What about your rent? He's not being fair."

Lynne reached for Noel's arm. "Hang on! Let me explain. Damien has asked me to spend my afternoons and evenings helping the dance academy students, and he's paying me for that help."

"But, Lynne—"

"It's okay, Noel. I have enough money to handle my trip to Marta's big do and still pay my June rent. Working with the dance academy over the summer will get me through."

"You know I'll help you." He paused. "Wait! Why don't we get married this summer? Then you'll be living at the ranch. We'd need to delay

a honeymoon, but that would be okay, wouldn't it?"

Lynne pressed two fingers against his lips and smiled. "That's an offer I *almost* can't refuse, but no. Let's get through all the craziness of this summer; then we can talk about our future while we sit by the fire and eat Cook's pies."

Noel laughed. "You're suddenly in love with Cook's pies. I'm almost jealous."

"Maybe you should be."

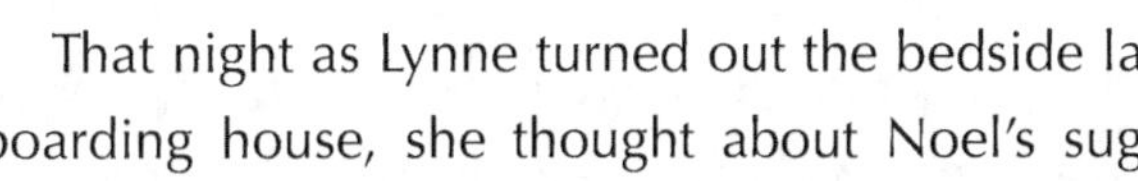

That night as Lynne turned out the bedside lamp in her room at the boarding house, she thought about Noel's suggestion of planning a summer wedding. Their crazy summer was already too busy with his kids camp opening, construction of the conference areas, Marta's wedding, her working at the dance academy, chauffeuring the dancers from France around the area, and working to restore her ankle for dancing another year. But…this fall…hmm. She smiled, fluffed up her pillow, and relaxed into sleep while listening to the faint sound of cars driving along Yellowstone Avenue.

The auditorium at Coontz Junior High filled to capacity Friday night as Marta began her last Bremerton recitals. In an effort to show support for Kersten as the new director, she stepped back from her usual opening welcome and remained behind the main curtain.

Kersten stepped up to the microphone, cleared her throat, straightened her sleek black sheath, and waited for the audience to settle.

"Welcome! Each year we look forward to sharing the skills of our dancers. This year is especially poignant as Marta is about to marry and move to Portland, where she is opening a new dance studio. We will miss her creativity. Her mother Elle, who has ably handled the nitty-gritty of the office, is retiring; she will also be missed."

The audience stood and clapped. Kersten signaled Marta to step forward and pointed to where Elle sat in the front row of the auditorium. Both waved to the audience as the applause continued on and on.

Tears flooded Marta's eyes as she stepped back behind the curtain to let Kersten continue her welcome.

"Our two nights of this recital are dedicated to Marta and Elle for their contribution to Bremerton and to dance. You're all invited to the dance studio for a reception after tonight's performances to say your goodbyes. But now, let's get started. Thank you for coming to our Wide

World of Dance and Music recital."

The usual but cute hitches in dancing done by the youngest students dotted their performance: dancer tears, children running off the stage, waving to their parents, facing the back of the stage, and bowing over and over again.

Mid-level dancers, aged eight to ten, often made the most progress but often received the least applause. Only parents who had attended their monthly viewing days could attest to their growth in skill and confidence; others saw competent dancers, but the cute littlest ones always stole everyone's hearts.

Kersten's gymnastic, baton, and tap students performed well, which bolstered Marta's confidence that she would handle the studio competently. Difficult as it had been to turn over leaving more of the ballet classes to her, it had alleviated a lot of apprehension. Kersten's skill, positive attitude, and ambition spelled success. With the four women handling the day-to-day reception and office issues, the transition would progress smoothly.

At the end of the recital, all the dancers assembled onstage. Kersten led Marta and her mother onto the stage and handed each a bouquet of yellow roses and wild daisies. The audience once again stood to applaud.

Two stage crew members walked out, carrying a long board. When they turned it toward the audience Marta saw the words Portland Dance Studio in bold, black script, encircled by a dark blue boarder. Musical notes and pointe shoe images framed the studio name.

Kersten stepped forward. "Your dance families wanted you to know how much we appreciate the way you have kept Miss Holland's Studio moving forward. When you hang this sign, we want you to remember

that we miss you, but we'll continue to support you as your Portland studio becomes equally successful."

Marta's knees threatened to give way. She reached for her mother's arm. That's when she noticed her tears.

Kersten handed Marta the microphone. She laughed as she wiped her face. "This sign is amazing! Thank you so much for your kindness, your patience, and your trust that we've always had your dancers' interests at heart. I grew up dancing in Bremerton. My years in classes gave me confidence as well as skills to continue dancing and to take over this studio. Now, Kersten will provide great dance leadership as Miss Holland's dance studio moves into the nineteen-sixties. Thank you again for supporting me during my years here. You will always have a special place in my heart."

Kersten took the mic back. "Remember our reception in the studio. Thanks for coming tonight!"

The dancers rushed Marta and her mom, hugging them, jumping up and down, and chattering loudly. The stage crew carried the sign off stage and slowly closed the curtain around the excited students, now rushing to join waiting parents.

The crew began their clean-up and locking down the auditorium for the night. After Marta thanked them, she looked for Kersten. Much to her surprise, she found her sitting backstage crying.

She hurried up to her. "What's wrong?"

"Nothing." She wiped her eyes. "I'm feeling relieved and sad and overwhelmed and happy, as well as excited and exhausted. Is that even possible?"

"It is. I remember the first recital I handled. I felt the same way. I think it means two things: you care and you're ready to take over."

The two women hugged; then Marta and her mom left for the reception. Their evening was far from over.

The practice rooms were a sea of dancers, families, and friends. The four wonder women of the exercise class had orchestrated the reception and brought in food and punch. As the people filed in, a huge basket placed on the long counter filled with cards and small gifts. The new sign for the Portland studio rested backward on the counter, leaning against the wall as a line of well-wishers took turns signing the back.

At ten o'clock someone blinked the lights, and the crowd said their good-byes and headed out. Kersten turned off the practice room lights. She, Marta, and her mom moved to sit with the four wonder women in the reception area while a crew of parents cleaned up the practice rooms.

Trixie clapped her hands and looked like she wanted to burst open. "Well, were you surprised?"

Marta stood and walked to hug each person seated in the office. "Surprise is not a strong enough word. Amazed comes closer. Thank you for everything."

"And to think we get to do this again tomorrow night," Kersten said.

"Yes, but you, my dear, are just getting started," Marta said. "I predict a long and profitable career with the studio."

Lily Rose spoke up. "Kersten, are you going to tell her or what?"

Marta looked concerned. "Is something wrong?"

"Kersten's promised to get up early and lead the exercise class," Frann announced.

She blushed. "It's the least I can do since these ladies are taking over the office tasks."

Marta's mom laughed. "You won't regret having them around. They'll be excellent at intercepting stage moms when you're busy leading your classes."

Kersten smiled. "I like the sound of that. Now all of you head home and relax. Let me close this place up."

Marta and her mom sat in Marta's house amid the packing boxes. Each held a cup of tea and looked through the cards and gifts in their gift baskets.

"Mom, I don't think I can do this right now. I feel too… I'm glad Kersten is stepping up and taking charge, but I'm also sad to be leaving."

Her mom smiled and reached for Marta's hand. "I understand. Let's box this all up for now. You'll have lots of time to read them once you've settled into Steve's house. I'm really proud of how you are handling everything."

"Thanks. It's your good example I'm following. I just wish Lynne was here. She's never seen my recitals. I bet she's deep into rehearsals. When she comes in a couple weeks, we'll take time to watch the recording together. I'm anxious to know what she thinks."

The Wednesday before the long Memorial Day weekend, Lynne left the dance company at three-fifteen and headed to the ballet academy to work with the young dancers. As she looked back on everything that had happened as a result of her being unable to participate in the Showcase, she remained excited. Damien agreed to let her teach the entrance moves for Khachaturian's *Masquerade Waltz*.

For the past three days, she and Jer demonstrated elements of the waltz in the large classroom. The lavish entrance to the sweeping music made a crowd-pleasing finale. A dozen pairs of classically dressed dancers would waltz down the aisles of the theatre. Their expansive turns and unison movements from the back of the performance hall slowly swept forward, approaching the orchestra pit before mounting the steps.

Damien spaced out the dancers, marked their starting places, and adjusted the tempo to accommodate the tricky transition from the aisles to the stage, where they formed swirling waltz circles. He promised to add a glittering chandelier to the set during performances 'to fancy it up'.

Dancing with Jer felt bittersweet. He was headed to San Francisco

to join the ballet company Bartley had formerly joined. While closing another door in her life, the move would open a new one for him.
She'd miss him, but she wished him well. He and Hannah would start
their lives together much like Marta and Steve were about to do. But,
who'd tease her or listen to her dance issues or bring her burgers and
milkshakes when she needed a friend? She'd be moving on whether she
liked it not.

Since Damien was disappointed rather than mad, Lynne knew she'd
keep her position in the ballet company. But knowing she'd have no
future chance for leniency short of her becoming deathly ill or someone
dying, she hoped life would remain settled. *Probably should start taking
vitamins to help me stay healthy.*

Helping coach the young dancers once again provided a wonderful opportunity to see the progress of the little girls she and Marta had
coached in Mrs. B's basement. It was sad that Brenda had moved away.
She'd been such a firecracker in the little group when all four girls were
together. *I sure hope she's still dancing.*

Like their older counterparts, they were excited to learn popular
dances created before they were born. Damien had chosen simple
dances from the thirties, forties, and fifties to demonstrate how much
dance changed over Madame Cosper's years as director of the ballet
company. The audience would enjoy seeing young ones dance the
Hokey Pokey and watching older students do the jitterbug and perform
the Lindy and The Stroll.

Tracy pulled Lynne's arm and dragged her away from the others
when class ended. "I'm kind of scared about our silly dance. I don't
want people to laugh at us."

Lynne bent down to be eye-to-eye with Tracy. "That's the purpose.
We want to make people laugh, so go ahead and have fun with it. I re-

member a time when I was your age and dancing with my ballet class. We were doing a funny dance. People were laughing. I was embarrassed until I saw my teacher clapping her hands and smiling. Then I knew I should just dance and have fun like she'd told us to. It ended up being one of my favorite dances."

Tracy nodded. "Okay. I guess I'll try to have fun, but what if people don't laugh?"

Lynne hugged Tracy and patted her back. "Believe me, if you use your arms and legs and do all the silly moves, everyone will laugh, and you'll be a hit in the Showcase."

Before heading home that evening, Lynne grabbed groceries for her personal shelf in the fridge and went shopping to get a wedding gift for Marta and Steve. The more she wandered through the department store and a handful of little specialty shops, the more confused she became. In the end, she settled on a blue backyard bistro table with two chairs that she had shipped as a gift from herself and Noel. Hopefully, he'd make the trip with her.

Once she arrived in Bremerton, she would be expected to help with last minute wedding preparations. Having had the four women take over the showers was a huge relief. What did she know about bridal showers? Nothing.

When Lynne opened the front door of the boarding house, she heard laughter in the kitchen. One voice sounded way too much like Uncle Leo, but that couldn't be. He didn't know where she lived. If he had, he'd surely have shipped her belongings to her. *Uh, probably not. The needs of others typically didn't make it onto his to-do list.*

Entering the kitchen, Lynne nearly dropped her bag of groceries.

Uncle Leo sat in Mrs. B's kitchen, drinking coffee.

"Lynney! There you are. You're a hard person to find."

"What are you doing here, Uncle Leo?"

"I was just telling your lovely boarding house owner that I'm on my way to Alaska. Catching the ship in Seattle next week. Decided to drive out, see the western US. I must say it's a lo-ong drive!"

He stayed for dinner and regaled the table with stories. "Lynney and I had a great trip after she finished her dancing gig. Drove through France, Spain, and Portugal. Tried all kinds of different foods and saw amazing places. Lynney, do you remember our stop at that beach in Spain where we ate tapas and I napped?"

"The place where you were pick-pocketed?" Lynne couldn't believe he flaunted being pick-pocketed and included her in his storytelling. She bit her tongue to keep from exploding in front of her housemates.

"That's the one. First time it's ever happened. You should have seen my niece in action, trying to get the police to help us."

Lynne tuned out much like Carol usually did at the dinner table. But when she glanced Carol's direction, she saw her deeply engaged in Leo's conversation. *She's probably looking for ammunition to toss my direction once Leo leaves. Thanks, Uncle Leo.*

"Lynney, Lynney." Uncle Leo tapped her hand.

"What?" Lynne tuned back in; the entire table group sat staring at her.

"I was explaining how we decided to go our separate ways in Portugal."

Lynne glared at him and set down her fork. "Excuse me. I just remembered I need to make a call before seven."

For the next twenty minutes, she sat in the common room waiting, listening to Leo share story after story. At least she'd saved herself from

sitting in the same room with him.

A knock on the door brought her to her feet. She opened the door, smiled, and hurried down the steps to Noel's car.

He kissed her as he started the car. "Hey. What's going on? You sounded really upset on the phone."

"My Uncle Leo found me. Said he drove to the Billings information center and asked about ballet studios. He told them he was looking for a professional dancer, and they sent him to Intermountain Ballet Company. The ticket office tracked down my information and sent him here. Now he's deep in stories of us and his adventures. I had to get out of there."

"That explains the phone call. Anything else you want to shout at me?"

"Yes—one more thing. Leo had the gall to say we intentionally went our separate ways in Portugal. Like I wanted to be near-penniless to walk and hitchhike hundreds of miles back to Paris!"

Noel drove on without speaking for several miles. "Anything more?"

Lynne laughed. "No, that's it. Thanks for letting me vent."

"Did I have a choice?"

Lynne kissed his cheek. "I guess not. He infuriates me so-o much. At least he'll be on his way by the time I get back tonight."

"You could stay over. Your wing of the house is always ready for you. We could fix popcorn, watch one of your smooch-y movies, and relax. I'd drive you in to the company in the morning."

Lynne inhaled slowly and exhaled with a sigh. "I'll think about that."

If she had left any of her clothes or toiletries at the ranch, she might have stayed. She hadn't, but her time with Noel relaxed her. Something about his faint drawl and his arm around her helped her unwind. She'd live a happy life if she never saw Leo again, but she should have at least asked him what he'd done with her belongings after he drove away.

Lynne unlocked the front door and stopped. Leo sat in the common room, chatting with James and Shorty.

"Here she is," Leo said. "Thought maybe you'd be back before I took off. I—"

"Leo, I want to speak with you alone, in the basement."

He said his goodbyes to the two men and followed Lynne. "I was just about to tell them about you learning to drive that funny French car we had."

Lynne didn't respond until she'd turned on the basement lights. "Keep your voice down. Sound easily travels upstairs. Some boarders may be asleep."

Leo nodded and sat on the arm of the couch. "What do you want to talk about?"

Lynne paced like a caged animal who'd swallowed a bomb that might ignite at any minute. Outside, she hoped she projected a calm person with a steady voice.

"First, why are you really here?"

"Like I said, I'm on my way to meet up with a lady friend in Alaska. I'm—"

"You can't stay here, Leo."

"I know. Just thought I'd see where you lived."

"You've seen it. Goodbye."

"Lynney, why are you so angry?"

"Gee, I don't know. Maybe because you left me stranded in Portugal. Or because I had so little money I had to hitchhike, sleep outside overnight in alcoves, and walk large chunks of the six hundred miles to get to the ship in time to go home. But it was too far. I missed it." She took

a deep breath and lowered her voice. "Maybe it's because you drove off with my dance clothing and my suitcase filled with gifts for my friends. Or did you bring it with you today?"

"You expected me to drag home the stuff you left in the car?"

"Leo, you *left* me in *Portugal*! What were you thinking?"

"I needed to hustle to meet up with my new friends. Plus, going to Portugal was *your* idea, not mine. And *you* hid my passport. I had to drive back over a hundred miles to find the hotel where we stayed."

Lynne pointed her finger inches from his face and gritted her teeth. "*You* left it behind. Did you forget hotels in each place we stayed held our passports? I had to give them almost every penny I had to get mine out of their safe. The owner left yours at the police station."

"Well, you could have—"

"I could have what? What should I have done, Leo?"

Mrs. B appeared at the base of the stairs. "It's almost eleven o'clock. My boarders can hear you two. It's time to end this conversation. Now."

Leo stood. Lynne watched him smile and saw he was about to turn up his charm channel. "I'm so sorry, lovely lady. Lynne sometimes gets this way. It's a family trait."

Mrs. B stepped into the room and pointed her finger at Leo. "She's not the issue. I know the true story of your travels with Lynne. You've come here and stirred up my house; I don't understand why."

"Well, I —"

"You've said enough. Lynne, is there anything else you want to say to Leo?"

Lynne glared at him and asked, "Where are my things that were stored in the car, and what happened to my ship ticket back home?"

Leo's eyes wandered the room as if looking for printed answers. "I left your bags in the car when I sold it. Got a good price; enough to buy the car I brought here and—"

"What about my ticket home. Did you sell that?"

"Not really." He hesitated. "I used it to upgrade to a suite. It was a really—" He stopped and shrugged.

Mrs. B walked Leo up the stairs. Lynne heard the front door open and close. In a moment Mrs. B returned to the basement. She opened her arms to Lynne, who stepped into her ample embrace. "I'm so sorry. When he appeared, he made it seem as if you'd invited him. Had I realized how upset you would be, he'd not have been invited to stay for dinner."

"It's okay. Everything is always about him. I pity the woman in Alaska if she doesn't see through his me-me-me personality."

⁓ ℓ ⁓

Sleep arrived slowly for Lynne amid toss and turns. *At least I spared Noel from his antics and stories. Leo would have probably tried to worm his way into becoming part of Noel's camp and conference foundation; that could have been financially disastrous.*

26

The second night of the recital and second reception went well with more cards and gifts, more signatures on the Portland sign, and more tearful thanks and good-byes. Marta and her mom used the rest of weekend to go through boxes Marta had left in her mom's house—the growing-up minutia from her school days and early dance years. Robert graciously drove down those last boxes plus Marta's dance studio supplies and the new studio sign and left them in the new studio as he headed to a meeting in Salem.

Over the following week, Marta and Kersten met at the studio, finalizing the transition, including meeting with the four wonder women to discuss office ins and outs. With everything moving ahead smoothly, Kersten planned to take two weeks off before summer classes began.

Late Thursday evening, Marta's phone rang. She checked the time: ten forty-five. *Why is somebody calling so late? Did something happen to Steve?* By the time she answered it, her hands shook so hard she couldn't hold the receiver still.

"Marta, this is Wanda West from Portland's Sunshine Realty. I'm sorry to call so late."

"That's okay. Is…is something wrong?"

"Yes. I'm so sorry. There's been a fire."

27

"The fire department called the owner, who called me minutes ago. The Antique Furniture Mart that shares the building with you caught fire. They're not yet sure how it started. Your portion of the building sustained serious damage. I wanted to let you know right away."

Marta pressed the phone tight against her ear but stopped hearing what Wanda was saying.

"Marta? Are you still there?"

"Yes. How bad did you say it was?"

"The owner told me it's bad, but I don't know any details. I'll check at first light and call you. I am so-o sorry."

"Should I come down?"

"Honey, let me check it out. We can decide when I call you back."

"Thank you for letting me know. I'll be waiting to hear from you."

Marta hung up the phone and paced back and forth. *Should I wake up Mom? No, she needs her sleep; a few hours won't matter. What did the fire damage? How bad is bad? What do I do now?*

After what seemed like hours of walking, she sank onto the couch. Her eyes, stinging with fatigue, drifted shut.

Car lights crossed her front window as tires crunched against the rocks in the driveway. She blinked. Pale streaks of dawn crept in her east-facing windows. A car engine shut off. Jumping up, she hurried to the window. Steve stepped out and stretched.

Barefoot and in her night clothes, Marta flew out the door and grabbed him.

He staggered backward at the impact of her body against his. "Hey!"

She started sobbing. Small whimpers escaped her lips. "There's been a fire at the studio."

"Which studio?"

"The Portland one. Wanda called me last night. She'll call back once she knows how bad it is."

Steve wrapped his arm snugly around her and let her cry as he walked her into the house. He grabbed a blanket off the couch and tucked it around her after he guided her to sit down on the messy covers. "Start at the beginning."

Marta rambled on and on, working through what she'd done in the new space and what Wanda had shared.

"Have you called your mom?"

She nodded and inhaled a ragged breath. Then she looked up. Her eyes widened. "Wait! You're here! When did you get back?"

He smiled and kissed her. "Late last night. I drove straight here. I see you've been moving in. It's about time!"

She tried to laugh but didn't quite succeed. "Don't worry. I'll get everything put away before… Oh, what are we going to do?"

"You're safe. My…uh…our house is fine. The rest we'll work out."

Marta pulled back to get a better look at him. "You're so tan…and thin and tired-looking. Are you okay?"

"I am now that I'm back with you. It's been a long time away. Thanks for the letters. They kept me going."

"Can you talk about what you've been doing and where you've been?"

"As much as I would like to, I can't. It's a strange, sometimes scary world out there; but now that I'm back, I won't leave anytime soon, unless it's with you."

"Having you here makes everything better." Marta looked around her slightly empty house. "Are you tired? Do you need to sleep? Are you hungry?" She took his face in her hands. "I don't know what to do. Can you stay or are you leaving again?" She stared at him and smiled.

"I'm here and I don't plan to leave. Don't worry about me. I grabbed a sandwich on the drive up, but I could use a nap. Maybe a couple of hours on your couch?"

"Sure. I have things I can do while we wait to hear from Wanda." She straightened the bed covers, fluffed up the pillow and kissed his cheek. Then she wandered off to the bedroom to close up and label the boxes of donations her mom would take to the thrift shop next week.

At nine o'clock, Wanda called and relayed the information the fire marshal had given her. "You'll need to come down to see the damage for yourself so you can evaluate your next step."

"That sounds bad. We'll be there as soon as possible."

As soon as she hung up, she called her mom. The phone rang and rang. Her breathless mother finally answered.

"Mom…" Marta started crying.

"Honey, any news on the fire?"

"Not exactly. Wanda wants us to come down right away. Oh, Mom…"

"Is there anything I can do?"

"We'll let you know."

The drive south provided ample time to get their lives caught up. After Marta shared the recital and receptions and her send-off, she waited

for Steve to share what he could about his time away.

"Although I can't talk about what and where I've been, I was most always safe as one of a handful of other reporters. We had our own armed guards and—"

"Guards? You needed *armed* guards? Were you ever scared?"

"Yes, to all your questions, but what we witnessed and reported was important. There is one thing I want to discuss with you, but I already know your answer."

Marta studied Steve's face without speaking.

"I've been offered a nine-month extension of the job I just finished. There's a hazard pay bonus that could set us up for whatever bumps may appear in our future."

Marta's chest tightened. "You told them no, didn't you?"

"I said I'd talk with you." He glanced her direction. "If I went, we'd only have three months together before I'd leave again."

"I don't like the thought of starting our marriage with you away. These last several months without you have been really hard. I want you here. I'll get a job as a waitress, even live in a tent rather than have you leave again. We don't need a bonus *anything* if it means you have to go someplace where armed guards need to protect you. I'd have been a basket case if I'd known that. Please, tell me you'll turn them down."

Steve smiled. "I will."

"There's something else, isn't there?"

He nodded and ran his hand down his face.

Marta studied the road without looking his direction. "Tell me."

"I called my mom before starting my drive to see you. Dad's feeling much better, but he's retiring. Harold Armitage will take over as Editor in Chief, leaving his position as managing editor to Turner. Dad wants me to assume Turner's position as assignment editor. I'd handle new assignments, deadlines, fact-checking, and monitoring reporters. My stint in Portland and my special assignment have more than prepared me for the job."

Marta continued to stare straight ahead, unable or unwilling to answer.

"Marta?"

Tears slid down her face. She brushed them away and turned to look out the side window.

"Marta?"

"I don't think I can talk about all this right now."

Silence tamped down any happiness about their reunion for the remainder of their drive.

They stopped at Steve's house and dropped off a few boxes, a delaying tactic before driving over to the site of the fire to meet Wanda and the others. Marta remained lost in thought. *What was there to say? Oh look! The sun's out? Let's go on a picnic; no, let's go see what's left of the new studio?* She shuddered.

When they were a block away, she saw the grey ash cloud. The smell of burned wood stung her eyes. She coughed.

As Steve turned the last corner, her heart knotted. Gasping, she first covered her face, then forced herself to look at the space where her new studio once stood. Ropes and sawhorses blocked off part of the street. A fire truck idled in front of the still-smoldering wood of the totally destroyed building. All the walls had collapsed like gigantic, blackened Lincoln logs.

A crowd of onlookers stood a short distance away, pointing and shaking their heads. A white-haired man holding a clipboard chatted with a fireman in a black uniform, pointing to various part of the ruined structure and writing notes.

Marta coughed again as she stepped from the car. She leaned against the passenger door and stared at the firemen walking through portions of the building's skeletal remains. Fire hoses sprayed in different directions. Steve joined her, placing his arms loosely around her waist.

Wanda West hurried to where Marta and Steve stood. "I'm so sorry. The fire truck arrived within ten minutes of receiving the call, but there was no way to salvage anything. What the fire didn't destroy, the water will have severely damaged.

Marta stared at the devastation, waiting to wake up from the nightmare. Bile rose in her throat. Where would she go from here? She'd lost boxes and boxes of personal treasures, her dance notebooks of choreography, photos, clothing, and her precious new studio sign with all the signatures and well wishes inscribed on the back.

When the supervising fireman saw Wanda, Marta, and Steve, he stepped their direction outside the cordoned off area. "Wanda, are these people tenants?"

"Yes." She pointed to Marta and Steve. "Roger, these are my clients. They recently leased this end of the building. What can you tell us?"

"Hawthorne is an old neighborhood. This building's probably been here since the thirties, maybe before. Walls are lath and plaster. Insulation appears to be cardboard and newspaper. Knob and tube wiring. My guess, and it's only a guess, is a rodent gnawed a live wire on an old lamp, and the sparks exploded into flames. The antique wooden furniture provided ample fuel."

Marta gulped and choked. Steve tightened his grasp to steady her.

Wanda made a note, then looked up. "Ask the chief to send me a copy of the fire report."

Roger nodded, turned to Marta and Steve, and shook his head. "So sorry about your loss here. Unfortunately, it appears nothing escaped the flames." He stepped back into the fire scene and spoke with members of his team as their securing of the building site continued.

"I've known Roger for several years. He's probably correct about the cause of the fire—not that it matters to you, except it means the fire was probably an accident rather than arson. Could also be a faulty baseboard heater. The insurance company will send an investigator to assess the damage after the scene is safe to enter. Probably be more than a month before they'll settle your loss claim."

Marta found no words; she nodded and started back toward the car. She and Steve sat in silence, watching steam rise in giant puffs as the fire team continued to spray down hot spots.

When they returned to Steve's house, the air inside bristled with tension and sadness. No matter what he said, her replies were single words. Looking for something, anything to do, he grabbed his keys. "I'm going to make a quick trip for groceries. Want anything special from the store?"

"No."

He waited for her to say more; when she didn't, he left. On the way to the store, he stopped at a pay phone and dialed his family home. He told his mother about the fire and asked her to contact Elle. "Marta needs someone to talk with. I think her mom is the best person right now. Tell her we'll return to Bremerton tomorrow."

Back at his house, it appeared Marta hadn't moved from where he'd left her. If only his phone had been reconnected, she could call Lynne or her mother or someone. Her silence troubled him.

The next morning, Marta ate the muffin he fixed and drank the coffee he prepared, but the normally upbeat, cheerful person he loved was

AWOL. Now his worry turned to panic. Not only had she lost her new studio, she'd lost boxes filled with treasures from her dad who'd died when she was seven. If only she'd talk to him, let him share in her sadness.

"Marta? I asked my mother to call your mom, so I expect she'll be waiting for you at your little house. We can start back whenever you're ready."

"Thanks."

"Do you want me to call Lynne?"

She shook her head. "I don't want to tell anyone about this until after the wedding. I can't handle a bunch of people being sad on our special day."

"Do you want to delay the wedding?"

Tears streamed down her face as she shook her head. "I need something positive to hang onto. Marrying you is that something. Besides, there is nothing anyone can do about the studio. We don't know what this means for us, so what could we tell others?"

"I'm glad we're going ahead with the wedding. Now that I'm back for good, how can I help?"

"It's mostly done. Maybe make sure we have enough champagne. Mom and I thought we'd have a brief celebration after the service. When we drive down to the studio, I expect it will be a madhouse of kids and adults; I couldn't find a way to limit the four women. Did I tell you about the sign they had made for the Portland studio?" Marta exhaled loudly. "How do I tell them that precious sign is gone?"

Steve watched her face close down. "We'll find another studio."

"And what will we have inside? Melted records and singed ballet clothes?"

"Your renter's insurance will eventually replace everything."

Marta face darkened. "NO! Not everything. Not my books of choreography, not my photos and albums, not my precious mementos from my dad, and not my spirit."

The next morning they started the drive back to Bremerton. Marta sat stone still for first half hour. Suddenly, her loud sobs filled the car. Steve pulled onto a wide spot on the shoulder and turned off the engine. "Come here."

She scooted closer and let her tears continue to pour. "What's the use? I don't think I want to start over again. How many times do I have to start my life over before it's useless or stupid or…"

"You don't need to plan anything now. Focus on June twelfth. We're getting married. Then we'll make the rounds to our receptions. After that, we may know more about the fire. We may feel like taking a couple of weeks, driving down the coast, wandering through those little seaside towns. How'd that be?"

"Fine." Marta wiped her eyes and reached over to caress Steve's cheek. "Give me a couple more days to work through this. It's so much to handle."

Steve covered her hand with his. "Remember, I'm right here to help. If my dad's not able to come to our wedding, I'll make a quick trip to see him. Otherwise, I'm not going to leave the northwest until you're my wife, and we leave together."

28

Billings, June

Thursday evening's dress rehearsal went well. Lynne loved herding the anxious dance academy students to and from the stage. With her youngest dancers, she made a point to emphasize moving quietly and holding their excitement until they were back in the prep room. Then they could dance around and chatter as much as they wished.

"I want to congratulate each and every one of you on your quietness in the hallways and most especially on how well you danced."

A young dancer stared up at Lynne. "But I turned the wrong way."

"You did fine. One time, I actually fell off an outside stage and landed in a bush."

The girls and boys laughed.

"Did you get hurt?" the little girl asked.

"A little. What I want you to remember is that *everyone* makes mistakes. It's what you do *after* that's important. I saw your wrong turn, but you kept dancing. That tells me you are a smart dancer. You didn't miss one *balancé* or any other turns. Now, this next part is the hardest part. You need to wait in here until the performance is over. I'll be taking other groups to the stage, but I'll be back to check on you. For now, get out the book or coloring pages you brought, find a place to settle in, and

someone will bring you a treat very soon."

Noel attended the dress rehearsal because he'd be away for opening night. He waited for Lynne backstage by the exit to drive her to his ranch for a late dinner.

They both relished their impromptu evenings, especially if they preceded Noel being out of town. His camp and conference areas were progressing. Investors supported his ideas and looked at emulating his facilities in their home areas. The post grad business and finance classes he's taken were paying off as his legacy of helping others took a giant leap forward.

Cook had set the table and lit candles when Lynne and Noel walked inside. He greeted them, set down large, tantalizing chef salads, and made his excuses, disappearing through the kitchen and out the back door to his bungalow.

Noel raised his glass to Lynne. "The kids were great."

"They were. I hate to admit it, but I'm looking forward to teaching them this summer almost as much as dancing myself."

"Can you continue to do both?"

"Not likely. Working with the young dancers is mostly proving to Damien that I'm present and accountable. After Marta's wedding events, I dare not miss any more days."

"About that. I'll make time to go to Bremerton with you."

Lynne let out a long sigh. "I was afraid you were about to say you couldn't go. It will be a fun break for both of us. We'll look around the area when we have free time. Have you ever stepped into salt water?"

"No but I've gargled it."

When she returned to the boarding house, she found several notes

attached to her door. Mrs. B had written down phone messages from her brothers and her Aunt Vivian. She plucked the one from Aunt Vivian and opened it.

> 11:00 PM
>
> Vivian called twice to tell you that your father had another heart attack this morning. This one is more serious than the earlier one. They expect he'll recover. Your mother wants you to come home. Please call Vivian. She sends you her love.

Lynne plopped down in the rocking chair. Her earlier elation evaporated. Wow. Her dad must have not been following his doctor's orders; maybe he was working too many hours a week in the hardware store. When were her brothers planning to step in and help? The last she'd heard, two of them were still out of work; surely, they could learn to run a cash register or stock shelves or haul heavy purchases to customer's cars. *Why does Mom expect me to come home? To hold her hand? Not likely. Damien will fire me if I take off any more time. The dance academy is counting on me to assist with the students during the first performances of the Showcase. I owe that much help to Damien and Gretchen since they are allowing me to miss the end of the season.*

She checked the clock. Eleven-forty-five. Should she call her mom? It would be almost three in Trenton? Would she be home or at the hospital? Had Aunt Vivian traveled from Baltimore to support her mom? What could she do even if she went home?

Lynne stepped into the upstairs hallway as Mrs. B appeared on the landing. "I thought I heard you come in. I see you got your messages. Come use my phone if you want to make any calls."

"Thanks. Can I make one now?"

"Of course. Vivian said she and your mother would be at the hospital. The switchboard will let the nurses' station know when you call. Here's the number."

She placed the call and waited for her mother to reach the phone. She didn't even say hello.

"Lynne! Where have you been? Your father is in serious condition; you need to come home right away. When can you get here?"

"Mom…I can't. If I do, I'll lose my job."

"Job? You call dancing a job? I call it a hobby. You're needed here. You must take over the bookkeeping so I can work in the store until your father recovers. How dare you tell me you can't come!"

"Why can't my brothers help out? Two of them live in your house and are unemployed. Surely, they could help customers and put together orders. You could certainly ask your assistant manager to handle the books for a few weeks until you find someone who can take over."

"Larry doesn't know anything about the bookkeeping. You took business classes in school."

"Mom, that was one high school class on personal finances. It taught me how to handle my money, not run a business."

"You need to get back here right away. You can take a class to learn what to do. It's time to give up your hobby and help your family—for once in your life."

Tension shot through her body like a bolt of lightning. "Hobby? I work hard, and I'm a dang good dancer. In the hardware business, I barely know a screwdriver from a wrench, let alone how to handle paying taxes and the rest of it. Why did you let me take ballet for so many years if you thought it was a hobby? Didn't you realize I was serious about dancing professionally when dad took me to auditions? If I don't have any talent, how do you think I keep my position here and was

asked to dance in Europe last summer?"

"Your dad *wanted* to take you because he liked your stupid idea of becoming some kind of dancing queen prancing around on your toes, but now you're needed here to work on a real job. Borrow the money from one of your dancing playmates and get on a plane; be sure to get enough to take a cab from the airport to the hospital. You can pay them back as soon as you learn enough. We'll give you a small salary once you learn to do what needs to be done. Plan to stay in your old bedroom. It won't take much to clear out the boxes we've stored in there. You owe us for all the money we spent on your dance classes."

"I *owe* you? I thought you said I could use the money you saved for me to take college classes?"

"Your dad made that deal with you. I never signed on. Now get off the phone and get yourself back home."

"I—"

The phone line buzzed in her ear.

Lynne stared at the receiver. Tears streamed down her cheeks. *She hung up on me. I didn't even get to ask how Dad was doing. She just hung up. Who hangs up without a reason?*

Mrs. B took the phone from her hand and replaced it on its cradle. "Is it true Damien will fire you, even if it's an emergency?"

"He might." Lynne sat down at Mrs. B's small dining table. "My helping with Marta's wedding pushed him over the edge. He likes Marta, but with Suzette gone, we're short on dancers until Damien holds tryouts this summer."

"Shall I keep in contact with Vivian? She said she'd call me with updates."

"That would be great. Thanks." Lynne hugged Mrs. B and headed upstairs to her room. She pulled down all the messages and put them in

her trash basket before settling into the rocker.

The next morning, she drove to the dance company, participated in warmups, then resumed her position at the back of the room during Damien's rehash of the dress rehearsal and changes he expected the dancers to make.

At three-thirty, as she headed to the dance academy to learn the changes the director wanted made by her students. Damien appeared in the academy hallway, carrying an armload of clothing bags. "Is everything okay?"

She tried to avoid his intense look. "Yes. I think the students did well last night."

"I agree, but how are you? You looked distracted in class this morning."

"I'm tired. I'll do better tomorrow."

Damien watched her face for a moment longer, then continued toward the door.

"Everything's fine," she called after him. As she started out the door, she muttered, "What could possibly be wrong?"

29

On Thursday evening, the ninth, Lynne and Noel drove to the Billings airport and boarded a plane to Seattle. Sitting next to Noel on the near-three-hour flight in the puddle jumper provided no opportunity to continue ignoring the realities overtaking her life.

She sat in the window seat, holding Noel's hand and absorbing his warmth. Although comforted to temporarily escape Billings for the distraction of the wedding, she worried about how she'd perform as maid of honor. Unless Marta could tell her what was expected of her, she was in trouble. She'd only attended one wedding in her life. Hopefully, Marta's four women would step in with directions when she needed to perform an official activity.

She wondered why she and Marta had attended so few weddings when most young women their age were overrun with friends' weddings. *Can it be because we live in a dance bubble where few women marry until they reach the end of their careers? If so, how will I handle being married and still dancing? Maybe Noel and I are rushing things if we assume we can be a normal couple.*

Noel kissed her knuckles. "What's floating around in the pretty little head of yours?"

"You think I'm pretty?"

Noel laughed and squeezed her hand. "Most of the time."

"Only most?"

"Yep. The rest of the time you're beautiful or raging mad about some-thing."

"That's me. A sweet, lovable maniac. Thanks for your opinion."

"Lynne, Lynne, Lynne. Are you still angry about Leo? Or are you onto your mother's hanging up on you or your dad's illness, or is it Damien's ultimatum?"

"I've merged them. Felt easier to tamp down one gigantic anger than four medium-sized ones." Lynne shuddered. "Let's talk about you and your projects. You look relaxed, so I'm guessing things are progressing well. It will be nice when we both have free time. I'm looking forward to spending lots of time at your ranch to check things firsthand."

"All's going well. Bring your old boots so I can put you to work. I'm having a weekend information meeting next month for potential inno-vators from around the state who want to copy our format. Hoped you might be my hostess-with-the-most-est."

"Sounds fun. But I'll need boots? Not very hostess-like attire." She rubbed her hand up and down his arm. "I'm so proud of you. It must be exciting to know other cities want to copy your idea."

"It is. Dad's really pleased with potential expansion of the program. My step-mom likes the idea of making it a tribute to my parents. I told her there'd be a building named for her as well. She's given my dad so much support these last few years."

Lynne leaned against his shoulder and closed her eyes. Noel chuck-led and gently nudged her upright in her seat. "Not so fast. There's one more topic that needs our attention." He reached into his pocket and drew out a small silver box.

Lynne watched him open the box. A bubble of excitement raced

through her. "Is this what I think it is?"

"It's a possibility. My father gave me his grandmother's engagement and wedding rings and suggested we use them because they're family heirlooms. If you like them, they're yours, with his blessing. If you'd rather pick out your own rings, we'll do it the minute we return to Billings. No arguing."

Lynne looked at the antique silver bands. The pair of rings interlocked with a silver notch. Each contained a diamond with a series of rubies surrounding the stone.

"He wants me to have these rings? Really?"

"Really. Try on the engagement ring."

The ring slid on her finger with space to spare.

"Looks like we need to have them sized. I'll take them back and..."

"No! Hang on." Lynne slipped off her necklace and slid the engagement ring onto the chain. "I'll give it back when we get home. But... I think you forgot something. Are you going to propose to me or what?"

Noel smiled. "Hm-m. I thought maybe since I provided the rings, you'd propose to me."

Lynne pulled her lips tight as if contemplating her answer. She squeezed herself down onto the floor by their seats on the plane and reached for Noel's hand. "From the minute you saw me, you knew I was the one for you. I made you laugh, and you liked that about me.

"It took me longer to realize I was the one for you, but I'm there now. You have Cook, so I know I won't starve. I have my own wing in your house so I know I will have a roof over my head even when I exasperate you. Will you marry me and make my life complete?"

Noel nodded, leaned over, and kissed her. "How could I refuse such an offer?"

The stewardess walked past and stopped. "Is there a problem? Did

you drop something?"

Lynne smiled. "No, I found what I could have lost. I plan to hang onto it forever."

They rented a car at SEATAC airport, drove to Bremerton, found rooms at a motel at Oyster Bay, then drove to Marta's house. A note on her door read:

> Welcome to Bremerton. Hope your trip was easy. I'll see you Friday morning about ten at Mom's. Head back to the right and turn up Lafayette as you pass the elementary school. It's easy to find: follow the balloons.
>
> Marta

In the morning after breakfast in the motel's cafe, they drove back to Marta's house and peeked in the windows. Most furnishing were gone. They took a few minutes to cross the road and sit on the huge log by the bay.

Lynne jabbed Noel in the ribs. "Told you there'd be salt water. Want to go wading?"

"Not really, but it's certainly peaceful here. I can see why she liked it so much; it's a great place to gather your thoughts or sit and watch the water." Noel checked his watch, stood, and pulled Lynne to her feet. "Let's head over to her mom's place and see what needs to be done."

Elle and Robert's home sat on the crest of the hill. The front lawn was a mass of colorful flower beds with white ribbons and balloons guiding guests around to the backyard, where the shower and wedding festivities would take place.

As they rounded the side yard, Marta ran up to meet them. "Thank

goodness you're here! It's so good to see you!"

Lynne smiled at the happiness beaming from Marta's face, something she'd seldom observed or felt from Marta recently. "Where's Steve?"

"He's running errands and should be back any minute. He'll pick up Noel, and they can go back to my place to avoid all the fussy things the four women planned for the bridal shower."

"So, I'm *really* off the hook for the shower?" Lynne took Noel's arm. "Maybe I could go with you and Steve."

Marta grabbed Lynne's hand. "You're not going anywhere."

As Noel headed toward the front of the house to wait for Steve, Trixie hurried up to the girls. She hugged Lynne, then stepped back with a concerned look on her face. "I hope you're not upset with us for taking over your job."

Lynne smiled and shook her head. "Go for it. What can I do to help?"

Under their capable direction, she set up lawn chairs and small tables for the dozen attendees and added a vase of flowers to each. Later, she would pass around snacks.

The guests were a jovial bunch, casual and chatty. Lily Rose arranged for a caterer to bring spring salads and fresh croissants. Lynne poured lemonade and spoke with the guests. As gifts were opened, she wrote down details so Marta could send thank-you notes.

The best moment came when she opened the gift held back to the last. The small box contained a slinky white peignoir. Her intense blush led to numerous flirty suggestions and continuous giggles.

"Wear it in good health," Lily Rose said with a slow southern accent.

"I will." Marta set the box aside and faced her friends. "I don't know what to say except thanks to all of you."

"I think Steve will be especially thankful for that last gift." Irene grinned. "Maybe you should model it for us."

Marta shook her head. "No chance of that." Her face remained rosy for the rest of the shower.

Shortly after the guests said their goodbyes, Noel and Steve returned. Marta hugged Steve as they sat in the backyard, talking with Noel and Lynne.

"Marta, honey, have you told your friends yet?"

"It will keep."

Lynne looked quizzical. "What will keep, Marta?"

Steve held her gaze. "Marta?"

"It's a long story."

Lynne and Noel listened to Marta recounting of the fire. With each new detail shared, they leaned closer together as if that closeness would soften the sad details.

Marta reached for Lynne's hand. "We're so sorry I didn't tell you sooner. There's nothing new yet about the fire. We thought the news would tamp down the joy around our weekend. From today on, we promise to keep you up-to-date. Just please don't mention it at the wedding."

Lynne nodded and wiped her eyes.

Marta sighed, releasing a tension she'd been holding back. "Thanks. It's going to be a wait and see for at least another month.

Lynne perked up. "There's one thing I can do for you. I'll make copies of all our dance programs and photos. Maybe Steve can locate news articles about the ballet company."

Steve nodded. "Absolutely! I'm already checking the newspaper morgue."

Lynne reached for Noel's hand and looked toward Marta. "Since we're sharing important stuff *before* the wedding, I guess it's my turn. "My dad had another heart attack this past week. It's more serious than his earlier one, but it appears he'll recover. My Aunt Vivian will let me know if his condition changes."

"Oh, Lynne. Do you need to go, I mean, you can if—"

"No. Right now, your wedding is most important to me. I can't let you get married without being here to make sure you two get through the ceremony."

Steve's parents arrived on the late afternoon train and took a taxi straight to Elle and Robert's place so his dad could rest. They had return tickets on the first train back to Billings after the wedding. That was the only way the doctor would approve his attending the wedding.

After supper, Quentin pulled Steve aside. "Son, I'm still shocked about the studio fire. How are you both coping?"

"Marta's a mess, but we're managing. No decision on what we'll do next."

"Are you still planning to stay in Portland?"

"We don't know. Like I said, we're not making any decisions right now. We want to enjoy our wedding with friends and family."

"Maybe a change of place would help. Have you thought anymore about returning to Montana? That job at the newspaper is still open."

Steve shook his head. "Marta and I need time to work through our plans without you pressuring me to return to the paper."

Quentin nodded. "I'm not pressuring you, son, I'm offering a suggestion."

Steve placed his hand on his father's shoulder. "Now's not the time." He walked back to Marta just as Lynne and Noel appeared to be leaving.

"Heading out so soon?"

Noel reached out to shake Steve's hand. "Lynne's taking me on a tour of Bremerton."

Steve chuckled. "After *that* five minutes, what do you have planned?"

"Hey!" Marta put her hands on her hips in mock irritation. "You're talking about my hometown. It will take at least ten minutes to drive through town and another ten to visit the city park."

⁓

Lynne and Noel wandered off and ended up sitting on a bench in the city park. People putt-putted past in their pleasure boats, soaking up the last rays of the day's sunshine.

Noel stretched his legs and put his arm around Lynne. "I wonder why Marta or Steve didn't tell you about the fire earlier?"

"Marta lost so much; it must be really hard for her to talk about. Who knows what her insurance will cover, if anything."

Noel reached for Lynne's hand. "What about you and your problem? Do you plan to call your mother?"

"I don't know. She doesn't understand me or my passion about dancing. She doesn't care about what's important to me. I love my dad, and I want him to get well more than anything, but my going back there won't help that happen. She doesn't care that much about him either, or she'd use the resources she has right in front of her. My two lazy brothers could do more in the hardware store than I could. She wants me to do bookkeeping; I don't even know how. She offered to pay me a few dollars *after* I learned. And she expects me to borrow the money to pay my own way back. What she *really* wants is for me to be who *she* wants me to be, not who I am." She sighed. "I hate to admit it, but it hurts to not talk with her or be there for my dad. I wish she loved me just for me."

Noel kissed her forehead. "Know that I support whatever you decide to do."

30

*S*unshine continued through the day of the wedding. The intimate setting invited guests to sit in small groups around white, cloth-covered tables. Decorative paper fans on each table provided relief from the heat of the afternoon sun.

Lynne helped Marta with her veil and handed her the bridal bouquet of wildflowers and amber-colored roses. At the last moment, she handed her a circle pin of three dancers. "Remember the pins Bartley gave us? I wasn't sure if you still had yours, so I'm letting you borrow mine."

Marta reached into the pocket of her gown and pulled out an identical pin. "I did, but I'll carry both of them. Thanks, Lynne."

Just then Marta's mom knocked on the bedroom door. "Ready to get married?"

Marta nodded, hugged Lynne, then followed her mother outside.

Robert's grassy paths between his flower beds lent themselves to wide aisles. The four wonder women had lined each with tall planters of daisies wrapped with amber and silver bows.

Looking ahead, Marta saw Steve standing beneath an archway, smiling as she walked closer and closer. A lightness spread through her as she swallowed down a laugh their guests would never understand. *In the next few moments, everything in my life will change. Regardless of what happens with the dance studio, I know we'll be a great team and work out whatever issues come our way.*

Steve and Marta held hands under the white arch as the minister began the service. A violinist played as he spoke. Lynne watched and listened, thinking ahead to when she'd be the bride. When the minister paused, she mentally rejoined the ceremony.

"With rings exchanged, the couple will share their personal vows. Steve?"

"Marta, I've loved you from the first time I saw you. Even though you tried to ignore me, I eventually convinced you to go on a date. Since then, I've cherished every moment with you. I'll even cherish the times we disagree, because making up is always fun. I'll survive the times you work long hours, and I'm left to cook our TV dinners. I love your smile, your determination, your kindness, and the way you pout. Thank you for marrying me."

When the chuckles died away, the minister called on Marta. She inhaled deeply and watched his smile broaden. "Steve. I love you and miss you every second we're apart. I love you in sunshine and snow, through fire and disappointments. I love your tenacity and the funny look you give me when I can't make up my mind about important things—like what flavor ice cream to order. I promise to love you forever."

When the ceremony ended, the guests stood and clapped, then toasted the new couple with champagne. Steve grabbed Marta and twirled her around as she threw her head back laughing and wildly tossed her bouquet into the air. It landed in a flower bed.

After they made the rounds, speaking to everyone individually, they and their guests drove to the reception at the Bremerton dance studio. When they arrived, they saw the front of the building covered with balloons and streamers. Music flowed through the open windows and doors. Inside, well-wishers filled the classrooms to the edges: family and friends, dancers and their families stood with plates of food as caterers hurried to replenish trays on every counter and table. A basket with cards and gifts overflowed as a loving send-off for Marta and Steve.

It wasn't until the reception ended that Marta noticed the changes Kersten had made. In two short weeks, she'd painted the dance studio rooms, added new curtains, and reconfigured the reception area. Marta saw the posted permit to add a bathroom upstairs.

As Kersten began picking up stray paper plate and cups, Marta complimented her on the changes. "I like the new colors of the rooms and the other changes you've made."

"Thanks. I hoped you'd not mind."

"Have you found a ballet instructor?"

"I have, but she's only available two days a week and Saturdays."

Marta hugged her. "That's a great start."

Kersten's smile faded. "I'm so sorry about your Portland studio. As you've requested, I've not told the families anything about the fire yet."

"Thanks. It's a huge setback, but things will work out. Good luck with this building. I see you've started on the upstairs."

"Why wait? I decided to stay here and work on the rooms rather than take time off. My husband understands this is my chance to finally start building my career."

"You've done a lovely job enhancing the space, making it an even stronger first-class dance studio."

The newlyweds lingered to say their goodbyes to their guests before returning to Marta's mom's house to change for their drive to Portland to spend their first night as a married couple in Steve's house.

"How do you feel, Mrs. Mason?"

"Fine, Mr. Mason."

"Ready to take on whatever comes our way, even choosing ice cream flavors?"

"Absolutely!"

31

Portland, June

Wanda called Marta twice a week to keep her in the loop, but the investigation remained unfinished. "I'm sorry, hon. These things take time. As you've seen, they've not carted the last of the building away. Expect another week, at least."

"Thanks, Wanda."

Marta sank down on the couch. The boxes she'd brought into the living room remained unopened. Did she care whether she put her clothes away or not? Did it matter? So far, Steve walked around the boxes piled everywhere and didn't complain. *Maybe I'll stash them all in the garage for the time being.*

She leaned back, staring at the ceiling, letting the pressure in her chest take over. Covering her face with pillow, she cried until she fell asleep.

A gentle hand set aside the pillow and brushed her hair off her face. When she opened her eyes, Steve stood, smiling down at her. "Hey, sleepyhead. How was your day?"

She shrugged. "I haven't cleared away any boxes like I'd planned." She looked at the clock. Five-fifteen. She closed her eyes and shook her head to clear imaginary cobwebs. "I don't know what's in the house for dinner. Sorry."

"That's fine. Let's grab a couple of sandwiches from the deli and take a drive. I know a park I think you'll enjoy."

They drove past the charred remains of the burned-out building on their way to a main thoroughfare. Steve slowed the car as they passed. Several long, blackened beams lay in a pile surrounded by small piles of debris.

Tears flooded Marta's eyes. She looked away.

"Sorry, sweetie. I wasn't thinking. Still want to drive to the park?"

Marta nodded. "It's okay." She kept her face turned away until they left their neighborhood.

The main roadway took them west to Washington Park, one of Portland's oldest. They wound past manicured gardens, a statue of Sacajawea, and a tall, slender granite shaft commemorating Lewis and Clark's journey to the west coast. Families sat on blankets, enjoying the last rays of sunshine. They found a bench under a tree to sit and eat their sandwiches in silence.

Even though it was dark when they drove home, Steve avoided the street where the dance studio would have been. Marta's intense quietness worried him. There had to be some way to distract her or at least help her move on.

The next day, when Steve returned from the newspaper office, he carried a small cardboard box. "I found more articles about the ballet company, ones Lynne might not have seen. I made both of you copies."

"I thought you were waiting to do that when we went to Billings for the reception."

He kissed her and twirled a pretend handlebar moustache. "Ha, ha, ha, I have my ways!"

She smiled as he handed the box to her. It contained photocopies of news articles dating back to the nineteen forties, as well as reprinted black and white photos. "This is amazing. Thanks. I'll start looking through them tomorrow, after—"

Steve sat beside her and held her as she cried. He'd hoped the contents of the box might help her regain a sense of calm. At least he'd tried.

Putting away belongings and working through the box Steve brought from the newspaper morgue gave Marta two days of distractions. During the same time, Steve completed his exit from the special investigative unit and extended his vacation for an additional week. They both needed a chance to find some peace, so Steve made a plan.

Each afternoon when they'd finished chores together, they drove out to explore parks in and around Portland. They walked along forest trails with bridges crossing streams and waterfalls, viewed old moss-covered stone buildings, and laughed when they met grazing cows along one trail. They visited the zoo and drove to an extinct cinder cone for a stunning view of the city and its meandering rivers.

After each outing, Steve noticed Marta returning to her old self. She smiled more and laughed at his jokes more. She talked more with him about articles in the paper or things they heard on the radio.

With the boxes put away, the house once again became a place of calm. They spent time together, enjoying the mild summer weather while continuing to explore Portland. Slowly her sadness and tension dissolved, replaced by moments of looking ahead instead of reexamining her losses. Time began working its magic.

32

Billings, June

Another reception on another sunny afternoon gave Marta and Steve a chance to reconnect with their Billings friends and work associates. The large group sat in the chairs on or near the patio or wandered around the Mason's backyard, enjoying the flowers and snacking on finger food and champagne. Many heeded the request that gifts be made in the form of dance academy or kids camp scholarships, assuring more children could pursue activities many might only dream of doing.

Quentin enjoyed the festivities but tired quickly. He excused himself to lie down, leaving Doris to hostess their guests. The reception settled down to small groups talking together until Lynne proposed a toast to the newlyweds. "May love and peace surround you each and every day of your lives together. Congratulations!"

Shortly after the toast, Steve and Marta made the rounds to thank everyone for coming and to say their goodbyes. After Doris dismissed the caterers, Steve and Noel drove to the ranch to look at the camp's progress, leaving Marta and Lynne time to talk seated outside in the swing rocker.

Marta put her arm around Lynne. "This has been fun. Thanks for helping me invite Mrs. B and the boarders. They enjoyed meeting Damien and Jer. I was shocked that Patrice came. I never expected our prima ballerina would socialize with us *corps de ballet* types."

Lynne frowned. "Why? She's always treated us kindly. I think she's happy for you; I know she's happy in her marriage. I wonder how her husband handles her holiday dance tours. Do you think she wants children?"

"Maybe, Why not? Women in other stressful positions manage to balance work and family. It just takes organization and getting by on less sleep. Have you and Noel made any plans?"

"Almost." With a grin, she lifted the chain out from inside the bodice of her dress and waved it in front of Marta. "Now that he's proposed to me, I proposed to him. We're currently on the same wavelength.

"Once the kids camp and the conference center are up and running, we'll set a date. You'll be the first to know. We're thinking around Christmas but after the *Nutcracker*. That means we'll have the week between Christmas and New Year's for a brief honeymoon getaway."

"You love the ballet company, don't you?"

Lynne laughed. "If you mean long classes, sore feet, rehearsals, touring, and constant fatigue, yes, I do."

"Will you consider teaching, after?"

"I might…"

Marta smiled and turned serious. "We had wonderful seasons together."

"Do you remember the day we met?"

"Of course, I do, Lynne. You took pity on me when my suitcase was lost. Madame was so angry I almost thought of taking the first bus back home. You saved me from total humiliation."

Lynne patted Marta's hand. "We've saved each other many times; that's what best friends do." She enclosed Marta's hand and gently squeezed. "I'm sorry about your new studio. I can't imagine how it feels to lose everything."

"It's hard, but I realized I still have a home and Steve, my mom, and you. The people in my life are what's most important." She hesitated for a moment. "What's next for you? Think you'll ever mend things with your mother?"

"I'm not sure. For the next few months, she'll be focused on my dad's recovery. I hope one day she'll realize my dancing is not a hobby. I've experienced too many challenges to step away without giving it my best effort. I also hope she understands that I wasn't qualified to do the work she demanded that I take over."

Marta nodded.

"I'm going to send you a ticket for a front row seat when, *not if*, I become a soloist. So, keep your bag packed."

"I know it will happen. If you can make your way over six hundred miles alone, through foreign countries where you didn't speak or understand the languages, with almost no money, you can certainly become a soloist."

Marta stood and pulled Lynne to her feet. "We'll go back to Portland tomorrow, have a small reception with Steve's new friends, and move ahead as best we can. We're postponing our honeymoon until the fire details get settled. I'll let you know when and how it all works out."

Lynne hugged Marta. "Life has given us a lot of challenges, but we've survived."

"I hope you know you've been important to me in ways you probably never knew, even from far away Montana. I often look back on the times I felt my life shattering and had no idea how to gather the pieces. You were always there with help or a sarcastic joke to keep me moving. Your support helped me turn many horribly depressing moments into small, manageable heartaches. I owe you so-o much."

Lynne chuckled. "I was just thinking the same thing about you. My mom's lack of support made me question who I was and even made me wonder if she was right. Did I stay with the ballet company because I didn't want to take on family responsibility or because I had enough talent to become a soloist. It wasn't until Cheryl, a total stranger, selected me for her tour that I realized I had enough talent to keep dancing."

The young women hugged for a long moment. When they separated both had tears in their eyes. They started to laugh. "Some things never change."

33

Portland, July

Marta grabbed the phone on the third ring. "Hello?"

"Marta? It's Damien Black. Do you have a minute to speak with me?"

"Of course."

"I'm looking to expand the company and will be in Portland in two weeks, auditioning for dancers. Would you consider joining my selection team?"

"Me?"

"Damen laughed. "You sound surprised."

"I'm honored you'd think of me."

"That sounds like a yes to me. Since you know our company and have experience teaching dancers, I thought you'd make a great addition to our interview team. I need a young person's perspective as we move forward."

"Thanks. What do you want me to look for?"

"I'll send you the detailed list, but add your own criteria. I look forward to working with you again,"

"Thank you, Damien."

⌒⌒

The rest of the day, Marta's spirits soared. She scurried around the

house, dancing as she emptied the last boxes she'd stored in the garage. Next, she whipped up Steve's favorite dinner and arranged fresh flowers from the yard in a cut glass vase they'd received as a wedding gift.

When Steve returned home, he found her humming in the kitchen as she finished preparing a fresh vegetable salad. He walked up behind her and slid his arms around her waist "How's the most beautiful woman in my world?"

Marta spun around to hug him. "I'm wonderful. You will never in a hundred years, no a thousand years, guess who called me today?"

"The Queen of England?"

"Better. Damien Black. He wants me to join his interview team when they come to Portland to audition dancers."

Steve picked her up and spun her around, nearly bumping into the kitchen table. "That's wonderful news! He knows talent when he sees it."

Marta blushed. "I can hardly wait."

The morning of the auditions, Marta fussed over what to wear. If she remembered correctly, the judges for her audition in Seattle wore dark suits. Her merger closet only had separates and most were well-worn; teaching dance didn't demand much when it came to fashion.

Steve watched her and laughed. "You are not going to meet the President or the queen, so just grab something. You are close to being late unless you leave in exactly…ten minutes."

She put on her knee-length white eyelet dress, added a lightweight dark blue suit jacket, combed her hair once more, kissed Steve, and hurried out the door.

Morning traffic was light. She spent the drive mentally rethinking the list of criteria Damien mailed to her. She'd added her own, including their physical attitude during downtime and their eye and facial gestures when resting. All spoke to their everyday attitudes.

Lynne once told her she had an emotional give away. "When you're stressed, you set your jaw like you're grinding your teeth. Then, when you're pleased, you pucker your lips slightly as if you're holding back a smile."

Marta started to answer, but Lynne had put her fingers in front of her lips. "I'm not done. There's one more. That little eye closing you're do-ing now means you're wanting to argue with me, but you're fighting it."

"Wow! It's a good thing you didn't tell me earlier. I'd have died of embarrassment. Now, I'll watch myself and try to change my ways."

Marta met Damien and his audition team in the ballroom of the downtown hotel where he was staying. She guessed right about their apparel but decided what she thought and contributed mattered more than what she wore.

The dancers' attention to details revealed much about where they'd studied and how much they knew about Damien's choreography prior to the audition. He valued individuality, follow-through on movements, and dancers who were confident enough to simplify their responses when asked questions. She also spotted the likely Suzette's as well as the company's future supportive dancers like Jer and, lately, Violet.

When the team met to discuss the dancers, Marta listened to their seasoned comments before offering her own views. Most favored the aggressive dancers. As one judge put it: "They show a strength of dance and character, a belief they are ready to compete for roles."

Damien turned to Marta. "What do you see?"

She straightened and felt her face heat up. "What you say is true, but consider also that a dance company is a special family. We spend a lot of time together, and we need to be team players. Dancers number five, eight, and twelve show a great deal in their faces when they are resting. They narrow their eyes and look at other dancers instead of staying focused on the directions. From my experience as a dancer, I believe those people may not be team players. I'd be inclined to consider asking numbers two, seven, and ten before offering contracts to the others."

"I agree with Marta on her selections, but I would also like to give number five another opportunity to show us who he really is," replied Damien. "He's similar in his executions to our current male dancers. Let's break for lunch and come back in an hour and a half to watch and evaluate their solos."

Damien walked Marta out of the room. "I appreciate your comments. You're a welcome addition to the team. Is there a chance we could have dinner together after the auditions? I have an idea I want to run past you."

"Of course. I'll let Steve know. Is there a problem?"

"No. I'd just like to speak with you in private while I'm in town."

Marta grabbed a sandwich in a nearby restaurant then spent the rest of her lunch break investigating the downtown Portland area near the hotel. In a pocket park, she found a bench that allowed her to watch pedestrians. Tall, short, young, or old, everyone walked at a similar nonchalant pace as if performing in a street-side dance. *Might make an interesting ballet solo. Could be fun to choreograph, if I had a dance studio. When the fire insurance is finalized, I'll need to decide what I want to do next.*

Wondering what Damien wanted to discuss moved back into her mind. If he wanted to talk about Lynne, she'd politely refuse. Anything he wanted to know about her, he'd need to ask her himself.

The afternoon dance selections ranged from well-known ballet solos to original dances. Their talent ranged from mediocre to excellent. By four o'clock the team selected ten of the twenty hopefuls to second interviews, which commenced immediately. By five-thirty, they'd chosen six dancers and made offers to them. Within the week, each dancer needed to decide if they wanted to take the offer. The hope was that two of the male dancers and one to two of the young women would say yes. If more said yes, Damien would have enough dancers to expand the company even faster.

She met Damien at seven o'clock in the fine dining restaurant in his hotel. He stood when she approached the table. "Marta. Always a pleasure."

"Thank you for inviting me." She looked around at the seating, the wall colors, and the art. "This is a beautiful restaurant. It reminds me of photos I've seen of the Rainbow Room in New York City."

"You have a good eye. I understand that was the inspiration for this room." Damien smiled. "I want to thank you for your insight on the finalists. I still have auditioning in Spokane, so it's hard to know what our ensemble number might grow to for next season."

"The company is gaining a great reputation. I know I appreciated being part of it."

After they ordered dinner, Damien turned serious. "I understand you've had a serious setback. That fire must have devastated you. Have you made any decisions on what you plan to do now?"

Tears floated into Marta's eyes. "Steve and I are trying to decide what we want to do. It was hard to lose everything, but people have been kind and supportive. My greatest losses were my personal albums and photos. They can't be easily replaced."

"Have you considered returning to Billings?"

"It's on the list of possibilities. Steve's been offered an editor's position now that his dad is retiring; doctor's orders."

"What about you? Would you consider returning to Billings if you had a job in the dance academy? We need a senior student dance instructor."

"You'd want me as an instructor?"

"I told Gretchen Ott I'd see you when I was in Portland. She wanted me to ask you if you'd be interested in joining the academy. She'd like to create a prep class to provide a bridge for older students who want to audition for the company. There'd be other classes to lead, different ages, different abilities. Since you taught kinders as well as older students, we think you'd be a perfect addition to the staff. You have good instincts, so we'd also want you to continue as part of our future selection teams."

Marta stared at Damien. "I don't know what to say. These are amazing offers. I'll talk with Steve about it. When would you want to know?"

"By the end of July. Planning begins then as our new dancers join the company. It's also our prep time for the academy classes, which begin after Labor Day."

July

With their decision made, they flew to their new town to look for a home to purchase. It only took half a day to find what they were looking for, so they returned to Portland by midnight and fell into bed, happy but exhausted.

Everything suddenly fell into place. They repacked Marta's boxes and loaded all Steve had accumulated. One week later, they'd move into their house and rent it until the final papers were ready to sign, probably another month at the most.

Robert and Elle drove down the remaining contents of Marta's little house by the bay. She'd decided she needed everything she'd left behind to make the house they'd purchased comfortable. The four set to work transferring everything into a larger rental truck destined for their new home as soon as they shared a last lunch.

Marta reached out for her mother's hand. "You're both welcome to visit any time. The new house has plenty of room. Maybe on your drive east this fall, you can stop in and stay a few days if you don't have a time schedule to rush you along."

Marta's mom grinned. "I do want to get back for Kersten's informal winter program. It's to be held at the Elks, where there's a curtained stage. She's created dances for every class using holiday music. The students will wear black leotards and dress them with holiday-colored gloves, boas, tutus, and hats. It sounds cute. She's very excited and proud to start a new tradition. She's certainly gotten herself organized."

"I knew she wanted to get more involved in the community. Is she continuing to send dancers to the navy hospital to perform?"

"I haven't heard, but it sounds like something she'd like to continue."

"Is she playing nice about the women managing the office?"

Marta's mom laughed. "You'll be happy to know she's kept her word about letting the four women handle the business side of the studio. I think she's relieved to be able to concentrate on classes. That competitive dance teacher she brought is adding a dozen more students. I know you wanted to keep the studio traditional; but everyone is happy, and it's helping Kersten pay the bills—which puts lease money in your pocket."

"I've learned not to look back and feel any regret for what pushed me to make my decisions and changes after Miss Holland left. Regret dilutes future goals."

"You sound like your father. He always looked forward. He'd be so proud of how you've handled leaving the ballet company, taking over Miss Holland's studio, the fire, the moves, and now marriage, the biggest change of all."

"I wished we'd had him much longer, but you've been an amazing mom. I appreciate everything you've done to support me, even when I wasn't especially loveable."

"I always did and always will love you with all my heart. Have a safe drive."

Steve and Marta waved until Robert and Elle's truck disappeared around the corner. He pulled her into a snug hug and kissed her. "Ready to get underway?"

Marta looked around the little house one last time, thinking about all the plans she'd once considered to make it homey. Luckily, she'd not made any purchases and could fully enjoy their current and maybe their last move in the foreseeable future. It would have been fun to explore Portland; maybe one day, they'd come back and spend a week, wandering around the various neighborhoods.

The drive was long and slow in a rental truck, giving them time to discuss anything and everything: meeting, their first kiss, winter at his parent's cabin, his time away, Marta's dance studio now occupied by Kersten, and their future lives, beginning as soon as they could unpack enough belongings to feel moved in.

Driving into their new neighborhood felt like coming home. The houses were ramblers with small, grassy front yards and large family-friendly backyards. The realtor had pushed them toward the newer neighborhoods, but they'd pushed back, wanting a more established area with kids and pets, basketball hoops, and flower beds instead of covenants and no parking on the streets.

They drove up and stopped in from of their first true home. They stared around them. A slow grin spread across Steve's face. "I think we made the right choice, don't you?"

Marta smiled and squeezed his arm. It's perfect. We'll still need to buy a lawnmower and maybe a porch swing."

He kissed her and chuckled. "Did you picture us ever living here?"

"Not really, but I think it's where we belong. It feels right."

The next morning before they began to unpack, they made a call and headed out to a local pancake restaurant for breakfast. As they sat wait-

ing, Marta smiled when she saw their friends walk in the door. "I think we pulled off the only secret we've ever been able to keep."

Lynne and Noel looked around the restaurant, spotted them, and hurried to their table.

Marta and Steve stood, ready to receive the hugs Lynne would naturally be giving out. "Hey! We didn't know you were coming to Billings. When did you arrive?"

"Yesterday."

"Great! How long are you staying?'

Marta and Steve looked at each other and answered in unison, "Forever."

*Good friends are like stars.
You don't always see them but you know
they're always there.
- Unknown*

Act 4 Reader's Guided Discussion Questions

What changes does Lynne face when she returns from Europe to the dance company in Billings?

What is changing for Marta in her Bremerton dance studio and in her personal life?

What are Damien's concerns about Lynne? Are they justified?

Why do you think Suzette is so antagonistic toward Lynne?

What qualities does Mrs. B have that supports Lynne and her other tenants?

What qualities do Noel and Steve have that support and interest Lynne and Marta?

How do the written letters in the story affect those who receive them?

What's Leo's motive for stopping in Billings?

How effective is Marta in handling her life-changing trauma?

Will Lynne reconcile with her mother? If so, who needs to initiate the biggest change?

Do you believe Steve and Mary are making good decisions moving forward?

What futures do you predict for Lynne and Noel and Marta and Steve?

Ponders

Have you ever moved? If so, what was the most traumatic or the funniest problem you faced?

How would the story series be different if they were set in current times?

If you had skills to become a professional artist (dancer, singer, actor, writer, musician, sculptor, visual artist, etc.) or athlete what would you want to become and why?

What specific challenges do artists and athletes face that differ from other people?

Special Thanks

Every writer deserves to have their own wonder women. I'm lucky to have *two* wonder women assisting me. Linda Lane edited the story, and provided great help on fleshing out details. Julie Mattern designed the cover, created the layout for the chapters and arranged the publishing details. Thanks, ladies. Working with you was a joy!

About the Author

 Paddy Eger is the multi-award-winning author of a four part ballet series: *84 Ribbons*, *When the Music Stops*, *Letters to Follow*, and *Act 4*. These stories follow the two, young, professional dancers as they navigate the ballet company and dance opportunities as they step into independence and adulthood.

As a former dancer, Paddy shares her love of music and dance as well as choreography and travel through her young adult novels. "It's important to look at the struggles as well as the successes the characters experience so they are well-rounded and human."

Eger's historical adventure novel, *Tasman* is the product of a visit she made to the Port Arthur penal colony on the southern coast of Tasmania. Through a combination of research and imagination, she recreates the story of brutal prison life, sharing glimpses into the deprivation and hard labor faced by inmates sent there in the 1850s.

Non-fiction is another interest Paddy shares with people who work with students. Her *Educating America* book and materials share easy-to-use ideas to involve students as well as classroom assistants.

In her free time, Paddy writes in other genres, reads, helps in classrooms, and travels. She and her family live in western Washington, but consider the world their home base.

Chat, Comment, and Connect with the Author

Book clubs and schools are invited to participate in FREE virtual discussions with Paddy Eger.

Chat:

Invite Paddy to chat with your group via the web or phone.

Comment:

Ask thought-provoking questions or give Paddy feedback.

Connect:

Find Paddy at a local book talk or meet and greet. Visit her website for dates, times, and locations or to set up your group's virtual discussion. For excerpts, author interviews, news, and future releases, visit PaddyEger.com

84 Ribbons—A Dancer's Journey

"A pure coming-of-age tale with moments of quiet drama *84 Ribbons* is about thriving despite the imperfections of life." YA Foresight, *Foreword Reviews*, Spring 2014. *DanceSpirit* Magazine's Pick of the Month, April 2014. "Any young dancer will find herself in Marta's story", Newbery Honor Author, Kirby Larson, *Hattie Big Sky*.

When the Music Stops—Dance On

Step into Marta's world

In the multi-award-winning second book, Marta struggles to regain her ability to dance and support herself at the same time stepping into adulthood amid unexpected challenges. Will she find a deep well of strength to meet her life-changing situations head-on?

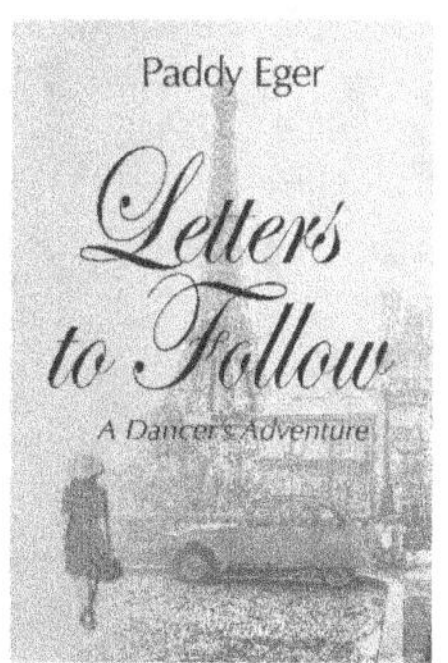

Letters to Follow—A Dancer's Adventure

Dance, the central character, enters the stage with a tour jeté and then piroutette's gracefully through the life of Lynne Meadows. This third book in the series glides into Lynne's world with backward glances at the fortunes and falls that bring her to the commencement of an exciting and grueling adventure as a member of a dance troupe traveling in Europe during the summer of 1959.

Act 4—The Continuing Story of Lynne & Marta

Dance, the central character, enters the stage with a tour jeté and then piroutette's gracefully through the life of Lynne Meadows. This third book in the series glides into Lynne's world with backward glances at the fortunes and falls that bring her to the commencement of an exciting and grueling adventure as a member of a dance troupe traveling in Europe during the summer of 1959.

Tasman—An Innocent Convict's Struggle for Freedom

In 1850, sixteen year-old Irish lad, Ean McCloud, steps off the boat, his legs in iron shackles, and steps into serving a three-year sentence at the Port Arthur Penal Colony in Tasmania. Falsely convicted, he must now survive the brutal conditions, the backbreaking labor, and time in the silent prison—a place that breaks men's souls. Follow Ean's adventures as he seeks not only to survive but to escape!

www.ingramcontent.com/pod-product-compliance
Lightning Source LLC
Chambersburg PA
CBHW060412310726
48976CB00003B/1025